THE AMAZING
TERRY JONES
PRESENTS
FOR THE VERY FIRST TIME HIS INCREDIBLE
ANIMAL
TALES

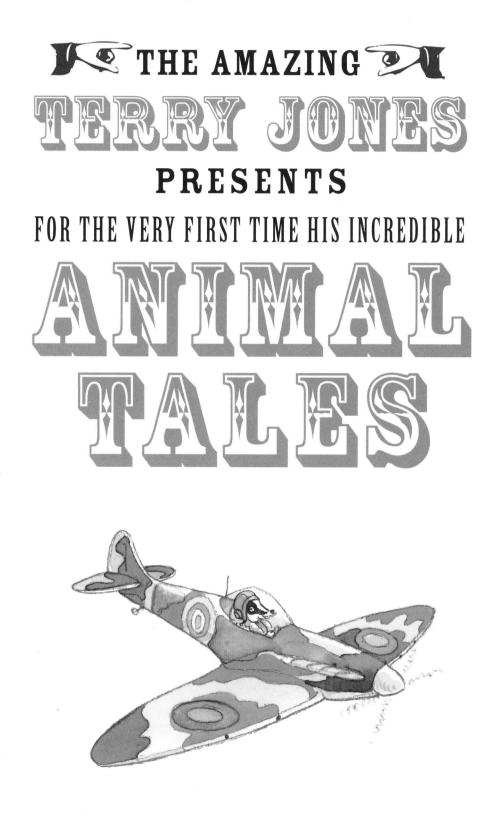

THE AMAZING
TERRY JONES
PRESENTS
FOR THE VERY FIRST TIME HIS INCREDIBLE
ANIMAL TALES

ILLUSTRATED BY
MICHAEL FOREMAN

PAVILION
CHILDREN'S

This edition first published in the United Kingdom in 2011
by Pavilion Children's Books
an imprint of Anova Books Group Ltd
10 Southcombe Street
London W14 0RA

A CIP catalogue record for this book is available from
the British Library.

10 9 8 7 6 5 4 3 2

ISBN 9781843651635

Design by Lee-May Lim
Typeset by Zoë Anspach

Repro by Mission Productions Ltd, Hong Kong
Printed by 1010 Printing International Ltd, China

CONTENTS

WONDERS OF THE ANIMAL KINGDOM

THE GOOD DOCTOR

THERE WAS ONCE A HIGHLY QUALIFIED DOG, who also had a great bedside manner. All his patients adored him, and – what's more – his treatments were more successful than any other doctor in town. As a result he had a waiting list that was the envy of the medical world.

But then one day Janet, his secretary, received a letter in the post informing him that the General Medical Council did not recognize 'Mrs. Barker's Academy of Paw Relief', nor 'The Tail Massage Centre' nor even 'Woofson College, Cambridge'.

"But I got a First in every subject I ever took!" exclaimed Scout.

"They seem to be quite adamant," said Janet. "They want you to close down your practice immediately."

"I can't believe it, doctor!" said Mrs. Nugent, as Scout was taking her blood pressure. "Why would they want to close you down when you're such a wonderful doctor?"

"They say it's not hygienic to keep a dog in the surgery," sighed Scout.

"But you're always washing your paws!" exclaimed Mrs. Nugent.

"Yes! And I never lick my patients, or jump up on them," said Scout.

"You're very well-behaved," said Mrs. Nugent.

"And I always do my business in the street," said Scout.

"I wouldn't make too much of a point of *that*," said Janet. "Would you sign our petition, Mrs. Nugent?"

"But of course, my dear," said Mrs. Nugent.

And within a couple of days every single one of Scout's patients had signed the petition to allow Scout to continue practising as a doctor. Janet then sent it to the General Medical Council.

Some days later, however, a man from the General Medical Council came to the surgery.

"May I leave my bicycle in the waiting room?" he asked.

"If you must," said Janet, and then she showed him into Scout's surgery.

The man from the General Medical Council looked around the room critically, as he presented his card.

"Do sit down, Mr. Catto," said Scout. "Now what exactly is the problem?"

"*You*," said Mr. Catto. "You are the problem. We simply cannot allow a dog to continue to practise. What's that bowl on the floor?"

"My dinner," said Scout.

"See?" said the Man from the General Medical Council. "The whole thing is unsanitary!"

"But you've seen my results," replied Scout politely. "They are well above average."

"You are not registered with the General Medical Council. Full stop," said Mr. Catto.

"But what about my patients!"

"They can go and find a proper doctor."

"But he *is* a proper doctor," said Janet who had not left the room.

"But look at him! He hasn't even got hands – just paws. How can he treat anybody?"

"But he's brilliant with his paws," said Janet. And Scout showed the Man from the General Medical Council how quickly he could tie a bandage round Janet's head with the correct fastening and everything.

"It doesn't matter!" screamed the man from the General Medical Council. "You have to shut down this practice today!"

At that moment there was another scream. This one came from the waiting room, and they all ran in to find one of Scout's patients sprawled across the floor.

"Aaargh! What a stupid place to leave a bicycle!" yelled the patient. "I think I've broken my ankle!"

"Sorry!" mumbled the Man from the General Medical Council. "It's just that it'll get stolen if I leave it outside."

While the Man from the General Medical Council was picking up his bicycle, Scout examined the ankle, decided it was only sprained, and bound it in a splint.

"Thank you, doctor," said the patient. "You are the best doctor in town."

"I hope you're listening," said Janet to the Man from the General Medical Council.

"He cannot practice unless he is registered with us," snapped the Man, and he stormed out of the surgery.

"Oh dear," said Scout. "What are we going to do?"

"Let's blow up the General Medical Council!" said the patient.

"I can't do that," replied Scout. "I have taken my dog's oath not to injure any human beings apart from postmen."

"We could just blow up the Postal Department," suggested the patient.

That evening, all his patients gathered in the surgery.

"Why can't he carry on?" said a woman who was suffering from Paget's disease (which, by the way, makes bones grow bigger). "I've never had a doctor who took so much interest in my case."

"We have complete faith in you, Scout," said everybody at once.

"So what are we going to do?" asked Janet.

"Let's hold a protest demonstration outside their offices," suggested one little old lady.

"No," said Scout. "There's only one thing for it. I am going to go round to the General Medical Council to reason with them."

And off he went the next day. He caught the No. 34 bus from outside his master's house, and arrived, an hour later, at the offices of the General Medical Council just off the Euston Road. "I've come to reason with the General Medical Council," he said to the man at the door. But the man at the door just said: "Clear off, Rover!"

"My name is Scout," said Scout, getting rather cross. "Dr. Scout."

"Scoot...Go on boy!" said the man at the door, trying to kick Scout.

"Please!" exclaimed Scout. "I demand to be treated with respect. I am highly qualified."

But the man just got a broom and started trying to hit Scout with it. This made Scout really mad. He growled and seized the broom in his teeth and pulled it and worried it, until he finally pulled it out of the man's hands, and then he bit the man on the leg.

"Ow!" screamed the man.

"I'm dreadfully sorry!" exclaimed Scout. But it was too late. The man had disappeared inside and locked the door.

"Mad dog!" he heard the man shouting.

That evening, Scout didn't even want to go for a walk.

"What's the matter, old fellow?" asked his Master kindly. It's not like you to turn down a walk."

"I disgraced myself at the General Medical Council," moaned Scout. "And now I'll have to close down my doctor's practice."

"Pity," said his Master. "You were making good money."

"Yes," said Scout. "I was hoping to be able to send you and the Mistress on holiday to the Bahamas."

"Don't let it get you down," said his Master. "You're a clever dog. You can always take up architecture or structural engineering."

"But I love medicine," said Scout miserably.

The next day, Scout was clearing his things out of the surgery, when Janet ran in full of excitement.

"Doctor!' she exclaimed. "I've persuaded the GMC to hold an extraordinary meeting to discuss your case!"

Scout was so pleased, he started running round in circles trying to bite his own tail. Then he licked Janet's face.

"Now stop that!" said Janet. "We've got to get the General Medical Council to take us seriously."

"Right!" said Scout.

The next day, Scout and Janet appeared before the Council. Scout wore his best collar, and Janet did the talking. When she'd finished, the Chairwoman nodded.

"Janet," she said, "we respect your concern for Scout, and we appreciate that his patients are very fond of him. But rules are rules, and if we throw the Rule Book out we are no better than animals…er…If you'll forgive the expression, Scout."

"Very well," said Janet, gathering her papers together. "We shall abide strictly by what the Rule Book says, if you will do the same."

"That is indeed what we intend to do," replied the Lady Chairman of the Council.

"Then we shall expect to receive, at your earliest convenience," said Janet, "the relevant pages from the Rule Book, where it states that a dog cannot register with the General Medical Council."

And with that she strode out of the room, and so did Scout.

Well I would like to be able to tell you that the General Medical Council allowed Scout to register the next day, but I'm afraid that didn't happen. In fact neither Scout nor Janet received any pages from the Rule Book that week nor the week after that nor the week after that.

In the meantime, however, Scout's patients kept coming to the surgery and Scout continued to be as busy as ever. And, strangely, the Man from the General Medical Council never paid another visit. Nor did Janet ever receive another letter nor hear another word from the Council.

"I think they must have forgotten about me," said Scout to Janet one morning.

"Maybe," replied Janet. "Or maybe they just don't want to rewrite the Rule Book."

THE CHICKEN CIRCUS

THERE WAS ONCE A FOX CALLED FERNANDO, who would go out of a night and steal chickens. Well, you might say, there's nothing so peculiar about that, because that's what foxes do, if they get half the chance. But what was odd about Fernando was what he did with the chickens that he stole. Most foxes would have eaten them, but not Fernando. No, Fernando *trained* them.

"I am going to create the most spectacular, fabulous and wonderful Chicken Circus!" he told his father.

"Can't you just eat the chickens like any normal fox?" asked his father.

"No way!" exclaimed Fernando. "These hens are highly trained! I've spent months getting them fit and teaching them circus tricks and gymnastics. You wouldn't believe how fat some of these chickens were when I got them…"

(Here Father Fox closed his eyes and licked his lips).

"I had to get them doing cross country runs to lose weight," Fernando went on. "They've all had to go on diets and undergo a strict regime of physical training. As a result these are now some of the fittest hens in the world!" He beamed proudly at his father, and blew a whistle. Immediately twenty hens piled out of the old disused hen-house that Fernando had found for them to live in, and lined up for inspection.

"This is Flossie," said Fernando. "She is our star acrobat!"

And Flossie the hen did a few cartwheels, and then went into a routine of aerial back-flips and springs that was quite breath-taking.

"And allow me to introduce Gertrude," Fernando went on. "Gertrude is our tight-rope specialist. She hasn't *quite* mastered the technique as yet, but we're hoping to get her up onto the High Wire next week. This is Jemima, one of our clowns, and Roberta, our lion-tamer…"

"Lion-tamer!" exclaimed Fernando's Father.

"Er…yes…" replied Fernando, looking a little uneasy. "At the moment she's practising with some field-mice and a couple of voles, but we're hoping to get her some lions any day."

Fernando's Father shook his head.

"My son," he said. "It is a wonderful dream of yours, this Chicken Circus, but I fear it is not a practical one. How will you ever get Gertrude up on the High Wire or get Roberta training lions?"

"Father!" said Fernando. "What is life without a dream? If we have no goal, what drives us on? And if we have a dream, if we have a goal, what can stand in our way?"

Well, Fernando went on training his chickens and teaching them tricks and circus skills, until he was confident he had the best troupe of performing chickens in the World.

"All we need now," he announced one day, "is a Big Top to perform in, some costumes and – of course – an audience."

So the chickens all got together to run up some costumes. Enid the Bantam (who was the most artistic) designed some posters, featuring Gertrude on the Flying Trapeze, and Rosie, the Rhode Island Red, and the speckled hen called Abigail went round the forest putting the posters up on trees and all round town.

Meanwhile Fernando had heard of a circus that was disbanding and wanted to find a home for their big tent.

"You can pay for it once you start making money," the old circus owner told him. "It's hard to find anyone who wants a big circus tent these days. I'm just glad to see it still being used. It would be a shame for it to be packed away and forgotten about."

So the day of the Grand Opening eventually arrived. The chickens were all in a state of great excitement, and Fernando had a hard job trying to calm them down. Roberta the Lion-Tamer was particularly nervous.

"My nerves are shot to pieces!" she confessed to Flossie, the star acrobat. "I don't think my Lion-Tamer's uniform fits me properly!"

"You look great in it," said Flossie.

"But shouldn't the hat have more gold braid on it?" asked Roberta.

"I'll put some more on for you," said Flossie.

"Where are the sheets of music for tonight?" cried Elsie, the Band-Leader. "I put them out on the music stands and now they've disappeared! Did Gordon The Golden Goat eat them?!"

"I've got them here," said Fernando. "I wanted to keep them safe."

And so it went on all day, with the chickens cackling and clucking with nervous excitement.

Then the audience started to arrive. There were plenty of forest creatures, as well as the bigger farmyard animals, and even a lot of people from the nearby town. All had come to see the opening of The Grand Chicken Circus.

When everyone was in the Big Top, Elsie's band started playing and the Chicken Clowns ran out into the ring to keep the audience amused, while the star attractions made their final adjustments and applied their last dabs of grease-paint.

But something was wrong. There was a lot of squawking, and suddenly the Speckled Hen rushed into Fernando's caravan. Her face was ashen and she was hopping from one foot to the other in agitation.

"It's Gertrude!" exclaimed the Speckled Hen. "She's gone broody!"

"Oh no!" cried Fernando. "Not today of all days!"

He hurried round to Gertrude's trailer, where he found her sitting on three eggs.

"Gertrude!" he exclaimed. "What are you doing?!"

"I'm keeping my eggs nice and warm so my little chicks inside will turn into fine strong birds and peck their way out of their shells and scamper around after me."

"But it's the Opening Night of the Chicken Circus!" exclaimed Fernando.

"I've always dreamed of having chicks of my own, and now my dream is about to come true!" said Gertrude with a far-away look in her eyes.

"But all those months of training and practice! You've got the High-Wire technique perfected! You even conquered your vertigo! You can't throw all that away!"

"Oh I won't throw it away!" exclaimed Gertrude. "I'll teach my chicks everything I know."

"But think of the show!" cried Fernando. "You're on all the posters as the main attraction! The Daring Young Hen On The Flying Trapeze!"

"I'm sorry, Fernando, I must turn my eggs over, would you mind going away?" said Gertrude calmly.

Fernando realized there was nothing he could say. He traipsed back through the mud with his head down, and a sinking feeling in the pit of his stomach.

"It's no good," he told the assembled performers. "We'll have to cancel the show. Our star attraction has gone broody."

There was a lot of sympathetic murmuring amongst the hens.

"You just can't help it once you go broody," explained Rosie the Rhode Island Red. "Hatching those eggs is the only thing you can think about."

"It's built into us," added Roberta the Lion-Tamer (who was now feeling much better now, since Flossie had sewed yet another gold braid onto her hat).

"There's not a hen here who doesn't know what she's going through," murmured another, and there was a lot of clucking and nodding of heads in agreement.

"But you've all worked so hard!" exclaimed Fernando. "It's such a waste!"

"I'll do it!" It was Flossie, the star acrobat, who suddenly spoke up.

"What do you mean, Flossie?" asked Fernando.

"I'll take Gertrude's place on the High Wire," said Flossie.

"What?!" cried everyone.

"But you've never even set foot on the High Wire!" exclaimed Fernando. "And as for the Aerial Ballet – why! Gertrude was doing a triple somersault from one flying trapeze to the other – without a safety net! You'd never make it!"

"I've been watching Gertrude closely. I reckon I can do everything she does so long as I don't get vertigo," said Flossie.

"Vertigo!" squawked all the other chickens in alarm, although most of them didn't know exactly what it was.

Suddenly Fernando banged his paw on the table. "No! Flossie!" he exclaimed. "I can't let you take the risk – with no safety net! It's unthinkable!"

But Flossie was not to be put off.

"Fernando," she said calmly. "You have worked so hard for this show. We all have. If we cancel tonight's performance, as like as not we'll never get another audience again. Word will get round that we're quitters, and we'll be finished in show-biz. We can't throw away all our hard work and all that sweat and training just because one of us has gone broody! No! Fernando! You *must* let me go on the High Wire and do the Aerial Ballet. I'll be fine – even without a safety net. You'll see! You'll be proud of me!"

A cheer went up from the other chickens, and Fernando held up his paw.

"Very well!" he said "Let's get this show started! We're half an hour late as it is!"

Elsie's Band was still playing, but the clowns had run out of jokes and the audience were getting bored with tricks involving eggs. Some of them had even started to slow handclap.

However, the moment Fernando the Fox strode into the ring dressed in his Ringmaster's costume, the audience went quiet. He looked so handsome and so commanding in his top hat and his red tailed coat, that every lady in the audience gave a sigh, and even one or two of the gentlemen.

Then he cracked his whip and six chickens acrobats ran into the ring and formed a chicken pyramid: three on the bottom, two on the next row and one chicken on the top.

The audience applauded politely.

Then Flossie ran into the ring, did a perfect triple somersault and landed on top of the topmost chicken acrobat in the pyramid.

Well, of course, at that the audience went wild.

"And now!" shouted Fernando the Fox through his megaphone. "Ladies and gentlemen, animals, insects and…are there any reptiles in the audience?

A couple of lizards raised their legs.

"…and reptiles," continued Fernando. "All the way from the five acre meadow and by special permission of Farmer Bailey, I have pleasure in presenting to you Adelaide the Dorking Hen, and her dancing cows!"

And in trotted eight cows with pretty headdresses arranged around their horns, and on the leading cow was Adelaide the Dorking Hen herself, dressed in blue with a tall blue hat with a blue plume in it.

She led her troupe around the ring, then they all turned, bowed, and started to weave in and out of each other as the Band played 'The Dashing White Sergeant'.

The farmers all clapped and the ladies in the audience murmured how tasteful the headdresses were and how they might think about wearing them too except that you'd never want to be seen in something you saw first on a cow.

And so the show went on. Flossie the acrobat was the star turn of the first half, with her amazing repertoire of jumps and back-flips, and by the interval the audience was entirely won over. They were even laughing at the clowns when they did yet another trick involving eggs. It was clearly going to be a huge success.

But everyone was waiting for the second half to begin, for they had been promised Roberta the Chicken Lion-Tamer and Gertrude –The Daring Young Hen On Her Flying Trapeze – with her Death-Defying Aerial Ballet (performed without a safety net). It was the climax of the show, and was pictured on the posters.

Well the time came for the lion-taming act. The great iron cages were brought on and the safety bars to prevent the lions escaping into the audience. Then Roberta entered the ring in her lion-taming costume.

"My word!" exclaimed more than one army officer in the audience. "Wouldn't I like to have as much gold braid on my uniform as she has!"

Roberta cracked her whip and six fierce lions ran down the caged run and into the ring.

Roberta cracked her whip again and one of the lions sat up on its hind legs and begged. The audience applauded. Then Roberta cracked her whip again and the next lion ran up and crouched down in front of her as if ready to spring, whereupon Roberta turned her back on the fierce creature and lit a cigarette!

Then she turned and blew smoke rings – one after the other – that all flew through the air, turned on their side above the creature's head and then fell perfectly around the lion, like hoop-la rings!

But before they could applaud, the drum started to roll. Everyone in the audience looked at each other expectantly: what was this remarkable chicken going to do next? Roberta took off her hat, bowed to the audience, then turned back to the crouching lion and prised its jaws apart with her wings. Then – to the amazement of the crowd – she stuck her head into the lion's mouth!

Well of course the audience roared and cheered and clapped. It was deafening. The lion, who had been used to rehearsing in peace and quiet, was so astonished by the roaring and cheering and clapping that it gulped and promptly shut its mouth – with Roberta's head still in it!

Roberta gave a pathetic squawk and the audience gasped in horror. However, Fernando was standing by. He leapt into the ring, and threw himself onto the lion's back. Then he gripped its upper abdomen and performed a Heimlich manoeuvre – which is what you have to do if someone is choking. Fernando did it so efficiently that Roberta shot out of the lion's mouth and crashed into the bars on the other side of the ring.

Roberta's feathers were a bit ruffled, but Fernando helped her to her feet, put her hat back on her head, and she was able to take her bow.

Then came the moment for the Aerial Ballet.

"Ladies and gentlemen, animals, insects and reptiles," announced Fernando. "We were to have witnessed the Death-Defying Aerial Acrobatics of Gertrude the Daring Young Hen On The Flying Trapeze, but unfortunately she's gone broody."

Everyone in the audience groaned in disappointment – except for a certain Mrs. Harris, whose husband had whistled in admiration at the poster of Gertrude, somersaulting in mid-air, in her scanty pink costume covered in sequins.

"However!" went on Fernando. "Her place is to be taken this evening by our star acrobat Flossie!"

The spotlight fell on Flossie as she bowed at the side of the ring, and then started to climb the rope ladder that led to the High Wire platform. As she climbed, Fernando continued:

"I have to tell you that Flossie has taken on this role at the very last minute. She has never before performed on the High Wire. In fact she has never before even set foot on a tightrope – let alone one that has no safety net! So when she attempts this death-defying feat, ladies and gentlemen, animals, insects and reptiles, may I implore you to keep absolutely silent so as not to disturb her concentration until she reaches the other side."

The audience gaped in wonder at Flossie, as she climbed up and up and up to the very top of the big tent.

It was even higher than Flossie had imagined, and when she looked down and saw the ring so small and so far below her, and the up-turned faces gazing up at her, she suddenly felt dizzy and had to cling to the rope ladder for a few moments.

The audience stared up at her with round eyes. Some of them were biting their nails, others were holding hands. Everyone felt as nervous as if they were about to do it themselves. And now Flossie had reached the High Wire platform and was about to walk a tightrope for the first time in her life.

"There she goes now!" shouted Fernando through the megaphone. "The bravest chicken it has ever been my honour to know! And don't forget, ladies and gentlemen, animals, insects and reptiles, Flossie will be doing this for the very first time and *without a safety net*!"

Suddenly someone in the audience screamed out: "Flossie! Don't do it!"

"Quiet please!" called out Fernando. "Please allow Flossie to concentrate. She is going to step out onto the High Wire at any moment!"

Another member of the audience screamed. The tension was unbearable. The drum rolled as Flossie took hold of the balancing pole, and put her first foot onto the wire. Everybody in the audience gasped. Nobody dared breathe, and then Flossie put her other foot onto the wire. She wobbled and took a step back. The audience gasped again.

"Please! Ladies and gentlemen, animals, insects and lizards!" called Fernando. "Please! Remain calm!"

Then Flossie took another step and then another. Then she wobbled again, found her balance with the balancing rod and stood stock still for a few moments. Everybody held their breath. Not a single person could tear their eyes away. Flossie took another step, seemed to sway... was she going to fall? No! She regained her balance, ran a few steps and then seemed to be getting the hang of it. Like the star acrobat she was, once she understood where to place her feet and where to put her weight, she became supremely confident. Halfway across she even balanced on one leg, span around, jumped up in the air and landed back on the other foot.

The crowd couldn't hold themselves back. They burst into applause. And then Flossie turned right around, and completed the rest of the crossing *walking backwards*!

The audience went wild. They cheered and stomped and applauded as Flossie reached the other side and bowed and waved to them.

"My word!" murmured Fernando to himself. "Even Gertrude couldn't do that!"

Well, when the excitement and the applause had died down, Fernando shouted into his megaphone: "And now! Ladies and gentlemen, animals, insects and reptiles! For your delight, Flossie will now attempt to replicate Miss Gertrude's elegant and yet *death-defying* Aerial Ballet! She will swing from one trapeze to another, flying through the air like a beam of sunshine! And may I remind you all that Flossie will be performing these feats for the first time in her life and doing it fifty feet in the air *without a safety net*! Such daring! Such skill has never before been witnessed in this or any other circus! Let's hear it for Flossie!"

And with that Flossie jumped onto the first trapeze, swinging herself and waving to the audience just as she'd seen Gertrude rehearsing it. Then she turned upside down, and clung to the trapeze with her feet. The audience applauded.

Then Flossie started spinning herself over and over on the bar of the trapeze.

"Ooooooh!" went the audience.

Then she swang the trapeze higher and higher and then let go, flying through the air like…well not so much like a sunbeam, more like a chicken. She couldn't stop herself instinctively flapping her wings a bit, as she hurtled through the air fifty feet above all those upturned face. But Flossie was in her element. She was used to spinning through the air and turning somersaults, and although she generally did it all nearer the ground, she told herself it was exactly the same thing except higher up.

As she tried to catch the other trapeze, however, something went wrong. She only

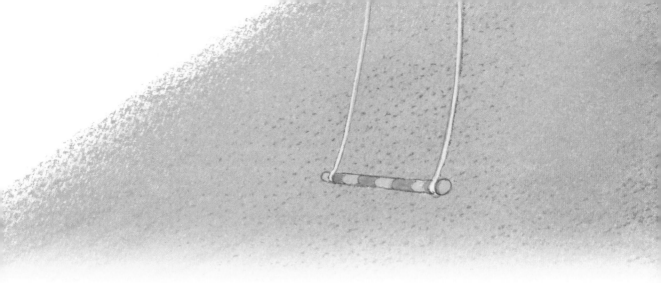

managed to get one claw onto it, the other claw grasped thin air, and she hung there on the swinging trapeze trying to reach it with her other foot, flapping her wings all the time.

The audience gasped. Flossie flapped her wings, grabbed the trapeze with both feet and suddenly let go. The audience screamed…But Flossie knew what she was doing. The trapeze was swinging back into the centre again and Flossie was thrown backwards towards the first trapeze. She did a triple backwards somersault in mid air and landed right-way-up on the first trapeze again!

The applause would have brought the house down if it hadn't been a tent. The band struck up, and Fernando leapt into the centre of the ring and yelled into his megaphone: "Thank you! Thank you! Ladies and gentlemen, animals, insects and reptiles! I hope you've enjoyed our show. Don't forget to tell your friends about Fernando the Fox's Grand Chicken Circus! Good night everybody!"

Well, after that, Fernando's Grand Chicken Circus became the most famous Chicken Circus in the World. They toured Russia, America and even China.

Gertrude's chicks all hatched out and became members of her Aerial Ballet. And whenever she went broody again, Flossie would repeat her performance on the High Wire complete with the Aerial Ballet, and Fernando would always tell the audience that it was the first time she had ever done it, and the audience never believed him but they always went wild anyway.

TIGERLINESS

WHAT'S SO GREAT ABOUT BEING A TIGER, apart from the stripes," said Tiger, "is bounding across the grasslands of Bengal, with a slight breeze on your fur and a fat buffalo in your sights! Yes! There's nothing like being a tiger!"

"But wouldn't you rather be safe and warm in your little burrow?" asked Mole. "Sitting there, still as a mouse, listening to the busy world going on above your head?"

"Bless my stripes!" exclaimed Tiger. "I couldn't think of anything worse!"

"But it's so safe underground," said Mole.

"Safe?" exclaimed Tiger indignantly. "I don't need to be *safe*! Don't you know that I'm an *Apex Predator*?"

"What's that?" asked Mole, who was rather frightened by words in italics.

"An *Apex Predator*," said Tiger proudly, "is an animal that preys on other animals, but has no animal that preys on him! What d'you think of that, little mole?"

"Oh dear, it sounds perfectly dreadful," said Mole.

"How could it be dreadful?" retorted Tiger.

"Well don't you ever feel sorry for the animals you kill?"

"No," said the astonished Tiger. "Should I?"

"Well of course," said Mole. "It isn't very nice being chased and then eaten."

"Pooh!" said Tiger. "That's another great thing about being a tiger – we haven't any time for sentiment! We're ruthless killers! By the way, did I tell you we can jump higher and further than practically any other kind of mammal?"

"No you didn't," said Mole.

"We can leap 16 feet into the air!"

"Goodness me," said Mole.

"And 30 feet across the ground!"

"Good heavens!" said Mole. "And I suppose you can run very fast?"

"*Very* fast," said Tiger.

"But surely you look after your families?" ventured Mole.

"Pooh!" replied Tiger. "Us tigers live on our own and we hunt for ourselves! We fight each other for territory and we kill a female's cubs if she won't co-operate!"

"You tigers sound like a thoroughly bad lot!" Mole finally exploded.

"Yes! We are! And we don't care!" roared Tiger. "That's what's so brilliant about being a Tiger! We don't give a fig for anything or anyone and yet everybody loves us!"

"What?!" exclaimed Mole. "Surely they can't!"

"Oh yes!" said Tiger. "We are what's called *Charismatic Megafauna*! We have immense appeal to human beings! We are the stars of any zoo. We can do whatever we want in the jungle! Nobody and nothing is safe from us! And yet humans still think we're wonderful!"

"Oh dear!" quaked little Mole.

"And now! I am going to do you a great honour! Even though you are so small, I am prepared to eat you as a snack before I go off to do some *real* hunting!" said Tiger.

"Bet you don't!" said Mole.

"Bet I do!" roared Tiger, and he pounced on Mole with his sharp claws. But Mole had already disappeared underground.

Tiger roared in disappointment and started to dig. He dug and he dug, faster and faster, but Mole could dig faster still, and besides he knew his way underground. Well, before he realized it, Tiger had dug himself into such a deep hole, he couldn't jump out. And he started roaring and roaring. Eventually his roars attracted the attention of some of the other animals, who normally avoided him, and they gathered round the hole and sat there the whole night laughing and making rude jokes.

And Tiger didn't get out of the hole until next morning, when his Mother came by and pulled him out.

WONDERS OF THE ANIMAL KINGDOM

ELECTRIC WOMBATS

Each wombat, when plugged into the main electric circuit of your home, provides the equivalent light of a 60 watt bulb. Throw out your old stationary lamp-stands and wall-lights! These little fellows bounce all over the house providing light in the most unexpected places! A must for birthday parties, rainy days indoors, and exciting bath times!

THE AMBITIOUS
CROCODILE

THERE WAS ONCE A CROCODILE who just couldn't get a job. "It's my teeth," he complained. "They're all crooked and irregular. Nobody will employ me with teeth like this."

So he went to his dentist.

"Open wide!" said the Dentist, and he peered into the Crocodile's mouth.

Snack! went the Crocodile's jaws.

When the Dentist's Receptionist entered the surgery, the Dentist was already halfway down the Crocodile's throat, and it was all the Receptionist could do to pull him back out.

"Well I'm certainly not looking in *your* mouth again!" exclaimed the Dentist, as he wiped himself down.

"But I've got to get my teeth straightened! Otherwise I'll never get a job!" said the Crocodile, and he burst into tears.

"I can tell you one thing," said the Dentist firmly, "there's nothing wrong with your teeth!"

And the Receptionist showed the Crocodile the door.

"Do you think my breath smells?" asked the Crocodile as he was pouring the afternoon tea.

"Could be," said the Tiger, helping himself to another crumpet.

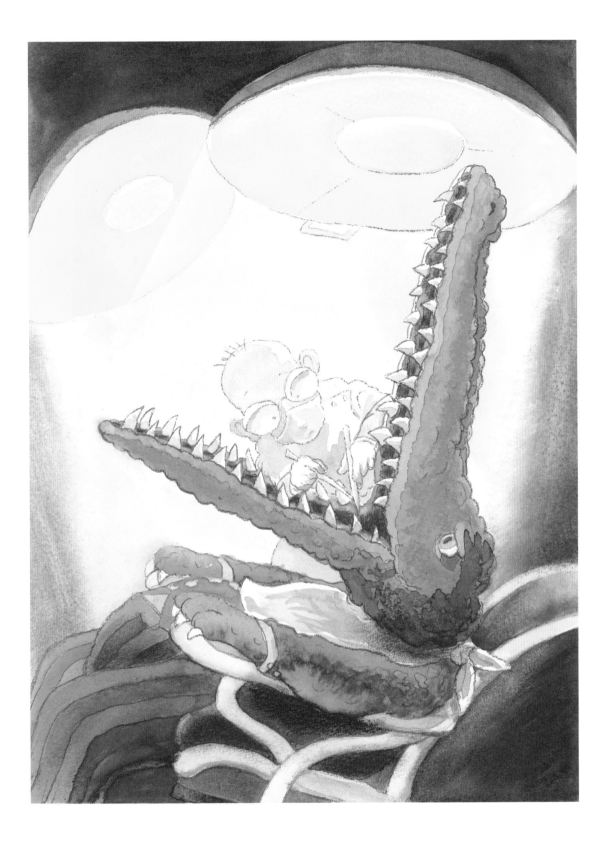

"Well I can't help noticing that people in the street tend to avoid me," said the Crocodile, "and if I ever get into a lift with someone, they always turn pale and start shaking."

"That definitely sounds like a case of bad breath to me!" exclaimed the Tiger and he ate up all the remaining 43 crumpets.

So the Crocodile went to the Chemist's and asked the lady behind the counter to give him something for bad breath. The lady behind the counter was a nervous sort of person, however, and when the Crocodile leaned across for her to smell his breath, she fainted.

"Typical!" exclaimed the Crocodile. "Trying to get served in this country is like trying to get snow in the jungle!" And he got so cross he twitched his tail and knocked over two stands of sunglasses *and* the shelves of stomach remedies. "And the shops are too small!" he roared, getting even angrier, as he knocked over all the tins of cough drops and throat lozenges – so they all went rolling over the floor.

By the time the emergency services arrived, the shop was a shambles.

"Look out! It's a crocodile!" screamed a policeman.

"Get the tranquilizer gun!" shouted the ambulance driver.

"What tranquilizer gun?" exclaimed his colleague. "We're ambulance men – not wildlife rangers!"

But the Crocodile had leapt off the counter and everybody screamed as it crashed about the shop trying to find the exit. Then it charged off down the road at a surprising speed for a creature that had just consumed an entire shop assistant.

"Perhaps it's my accent?" said the Crocodile, as he and the Tiger were watching football on TV. "I have this terrible crocodiley way of speaking. Perhaps it's putting employers off?"

"Could be," said the Tiger.

"Or do you think it's my colour? I hear there is a lot of colour prejudice in this country: perhaps they don't like green? Or do you think it's my CV? There's an awful lot of sitting around in swamps, waiting for my prey in it, which I don't suppose is the sort of thing employers in this country are looking for?"

"Listen," said the Tiger. "Did it ever occur to you that what might be putting employers off is your tendency to eat them?"

"Do you think that's it?" asked the Crocodile.

"I'd certainly never employ someone who might eat me," said the Tiger.

"It's just that I can't stop myself," said the Crocodile. "It's a compulsion."

"Then you ought to go and see a psychiatrist," said the Tiger.

So the Crocodile went to see a psychiatrist.

The Psychiatrist told him to lie down on the couch, while he got out his notebook. The Crocodile watched the Psychiatrist with his beady eyes.

Then the Psychiatrist started asking the Crocodile questions, and the Crocodile soon found himself pouring out his heart to him. The Psychiatrist was most understanding and not at all critical. Eventually he said:

"Your problem is that you're satisfying a short-term need. You need to re-prioritize! Look at the long-term!"

"Yes! Yes!" cried the Crocodile excitedly. "That's exactly right! I will!"

And then they went on, delving deeper and deeper into the Crocodile's mind. It was a most satisfying session in all sorts of ways, and, by the time the Psychiatrist's secretary came to tell him the next patient had arrived, all that remained of the Psychiatrist was his shoes.

The Crocodile was lying on the couch looking rather shifty.

"Where is Dr. Fonzella?" asked the Secretary.

"Burp!" said the Crocodile.

"The sort of job you need," said the Tiger, "is the sort of job where they *want* you to eat people."

"Good idea!" exclaimed the Crocodile. Then he thought for a moment. "But I don't suppose there are many jobs like that around," he added.

"No," replied the Tiger. "I don't suppose there are. But you could ask."

So the Crocodile went to an employment agency, and after he had swallowed the head of the agency and his assistant, the telephone rang. The Crocodile picked it up and a voice said: "Is that the Find-U-A-Job Agency?"

"Yeeees," said the Crocodile cautiously, not wanting to reveal that he had just eaten most of the staff.

"Do you have anyone on your books that looks like they might really eat someone alive?"

"Yes! Yes!" exclaimed the Crocodile. "I'm your man! I mean crocodile! I mean…" Here the Crocodile adopted a more professional voice. "Yes, Sir! We have someone on our books who will do exactly that for you!"

"Good," said the voice. "Send them round at once to Sharples Department Store. Tell them to report to the General Manager."

So the Crocodile hurried round to Sharples Department Store and knocked on the door of the General Manager.

"Come in!" said the General Manager.

The Crocodile peered round the door and smiled a crocodile smile.

"Whooaaa!" said the General Manager.

"I've come about that job" said the Crocodile.

"Keep out! Get away! Help!"

The Crocodile's face fell. "Is it my irregular teeth putting you off?" he asked.

"No, it's not that," replied the General manager.

"Is it my breath?" asked the Crocodile and he tried to breathe on the General Manager, but the General Manager hid behind his desk and shouted: "No! Your breath is fine!"

"Then it's my accent?" said the Crocodile sadly. "I know it's too crocodiley."

"Look," said the General Manager. "It's not your breath or your accent, it's just that we only want someone who *looks* as if they might eat people alive! We don't want anyone to be actually eaten! It's just to keep people in line during the January Sales!"

"I'll never get a job," moaned the Crocodile, and he collapsed into a miserable heap on the office carpet.

Now the General Manager of Sharples Department Store was a soft-hearted man, and he felt really sorry for the Crocodile.

"Look," he said. "As far as appearances go you fit the job to a tee. You scared me witless when you came in just now. Do you think you could manage not to actually eat anyone?"

"I'll do my very best," said the Crocodile.

"Very well," said the General Manager. "But the first person you attempt to eat, you're fired!"

"It's a deal!" said the Crocodile.

The Crocodile was given a smart suit, with the name 'Sharples' embroidered on the breast pocket, and a peaked hat with a bright yellow band around it. Then he stood outside the shop making sure that the queues for the January Sales didn't block the street or create a disturbance.

It was difficult work, particularly as he had to keep restraining himself every time he felt the urge to bite off some woman's head or snap up a child as an inter-meal snack, just to stop his tummy rumbling. But the Crocodile not only managed to stop himself eating anyone, he even kept his temper. And as the word got round the town that although he might look very frightening he was, in fact, quite friendly, people came from far and near to see the Crocodile keeping order outside Sharples' Department Store.

That year the January Sales were the most successful and profitable ever.

"Well done, Crocodile!" said the General Manager. "You have been a credit to the Store! Please accept this bonus!" And he handed over a large cheque. All the other employees applauded and gave three hearty cheers for the Crocodile.

Well! The Crocodile was so overcome with happiness that, for the first time since he'd been given the job, he relaxed his self-control, and before you could say "See you later, Alligator!" he'd gobbled up both the General Manager and Mr. Sharples himself, who actually owned the entire Department Store.

There was a dreadful silence. The Crocodile looked around at the shocked faces of the other employees, and realised he'd made a bad career move.

"Oh dear! I think I'd better be going..." he murmured. And before the crowd could gather their wits he'd run off and hidden in a disused pyjama factory.

There he thought over his life and ambitions and his hopes for the future, and realized that he was as far off achieving them as ever.

He sighed as he lay there digesting, first the General Manager and then Mr. Sharples, and he decided that perhaps, after all, he should return to his old swamp in the badlands and go back to doing the things that crocodiles generally do.

And so it was that the Crocodile never applied for another job ever again, and from that day forth, the Tiger had to eat his crumpets on his own.

THE TRANSYLVANIAN LIMPING BAT

This bat flies into your letterbox at night and when you pick the post up in the morning, it puts on a convincing performance of having a broken leg. However, once you have taken pity on it, tucked it up into a nice cosy shoe-box, it will revert to its true nature and become Sir Cliff Richard.

Only specially trained handlers can stop it from singing the entire score of *Summer Holiday*.

Once these bats get into your attic, it is impossible to stop them endlessly repeating the chorus of *Bachelor Boy* and your only solution is to demolish the house.

THE GOLDEN SNAIL
OF SURBITON

A LONG TIME AGO, THE FIERCEST and most powerful snail in all the world lived in what is now Surbiton. He was known as The Golden Snail of Surbiton.

Of course in those days Surbiton was very different from what it is today. Where the railway station now stands there was an anthill the size of the Great Pyramid in Egypt. The ants who had built it were as big and brawny as elephants.

They were also a rough lot, those ants, and would think nothing of holding up passing strangers and robbing them of everything they possessed. Indeed, in those days it was a dangerous journey to travel from Tolworth to Teddington, and travellers would make out their wills beforehand.

One day, the Golden Snail of Surbiton decided he had to teach these Robber Ants a lesson, so he called together a meeting of all the fiercest and boldest snails in the area.

"Who is afraid of the Robber Ants?" he cried.

"Me!" shouted one of the smaller snails.

"What?" exclaimed the Golden Snail of Surbiton.

"Well they're as big as elephants and don't care what they do to anyone! They're mean and cruel and they have huge stings!" said the smaller snail.

"Shame on you!" cried the Golden Snail of Surbiton. "No snail should be afraid of a mere ant! You will suffer the dreadful *ignominy** of staying behind while we rid Surbiton of the Robber Ants."

---

* Which is a more impressive way of saying 'disgrace' or 'shame'.

As he said this, another snail raised one of its horns and said "I'm not as afraid as the previous speaker, but I really wouldn't mind the *ignominy* of staying behind. In fact I'd prefer a little *ignominy* to getting in a fight with some giant Robber Ants."

Golden Snail frowned. "Are there any other snails who think like this?" he asked in a voice like thunder.

Several snails' horns were raised up and then a few more and finally every snail at the meeting indicated that it would prefer a bit of *ignominy* to the dangers of tackling Robber Ants the size of elephants.

"Very well," said the Golden Snail of Surbiton. "I shall do it alone! Alone I will teach these wicked brigands a lesson they will never forget! And as for the rest of you…From this time on I disown you all. As far as I am concerned, you are no longer worthy of the name of Snail."

And with that he spun around on his foot and slid off over the horizon.

It so happened that, in those far-off times, in the place where today stands the majestic Surbiton Water Works, there used to be a swamp full of deadly creatures. In it lived the Blind Swamp Lizard that had jaws so powerful it could bite the head off an elephant, if ever it saw one. There were Swamp Rats so numerous they could gnaw you to the bone the moment you fell in. There were Venomous Swamp Snakes and Poisonous Swamp Toads and the Vultures of the Swamp that hung circling in the air above, waiting for the dead things that floated to the surface. No! Take my word for it: the Great Swamp of Surbiton was no place for any living creature that didn't belong in it!

Well, you may be sure that the Golden Snail gave the Swamp a wide birth as he made his way towards the Great Anthill. When he arrived he knocked three times on the front door.

"Who's there?" demanded the Sentry Ant, sticking its gigantic head out of an upstairs window.

"It is I! The Golden Snail of Surbiton!" roared the Golden Snail of Surbiton.

"I can see that!" replied the Sentry. "What do you want?"

"I have come to challenge every single one of you Robber Ants to a battle to the death!"

"On your own?" asked the Sentry Ant.

"On my own!" replied the Golden Snail of Surbiton.

"You must be joking!" exclaimed the Sentry Ant.

"Far from it!" said the Golden Snail. "Take me to your Queen!"

So the Sentry took the Golden Snail to the Queen of all the Ants. Now if the Robber Ants were huge as elephants, you can imagine how truly gigantic their Queen was. She was the size of a Blue Whale! But the Golden Snail of Surbiton was undeterred, and he told the Queen of the Ants what he had come about.

"We ants have no quarrel with you snails." said the Queen of the Ants. "Why not let us get on with our business, while you get on with yours?"

"Your activities are getting Surbiton a bad name," replied the Golden Snail. "Travellers going from Tolworth to Teddington are now taking the long detour via Malden. Us snails haven't seen a half-eaten sandwich or a bit of apple peel in many a year! It is my duty to call upon you ants to cease your robbery and thieving or else face the Wrath of the Snails!"

"We accept your challenge!" said the Queen of the Robber Ants. "Do you have your army close by?"

"I have no army," replied the Golden Snail. "I shall fight you alone."

The Queen of the Ants raised a feeler in surprise.

"I see," said the Queen.

"The other snails said I would beat you so easily that they couldn't even be bothered to watch!" added the Golden Snail.

"Very well," replied the Queen, " you can fight our smallest and puniest soldier ant."

"No I shall not!" exclaimed the Golden Snail of Surbiton, "I intend to fight you all at the same time!"

"What?!" exclaimed the Queen, and she was so surprised that her tiara fell off.

"What!?" exclaimed all ants of the court. "You can't be serious!"

"We shall fight tomorrow!" said the Golden Snail.

A buzz of excitement ran around the court of the Robber Ants, and as it spread to the workers and soldiers and all the other ants of the colony, it grew into a sound like thunder and the whole anthill shook with the sounds of amazement, which quickly turned to laughter and mockery.

Well, the next day all the Robber Ants the size of elephants arrayed themselves in front of the Giant Anthill that used to stand where Surbiton Railway Station now stands. And the Queen of the Robber Ants stood in their midst, surrounded by as formidable an army as Surbiton has ever seen. When they were all in position they started to chant: "Where's the Snail? Give us the Snail!"

But the Golden Snail didn't appear. Then the Robber Ants started taunting the Golden Snail.

"He's not Golden!" they cried. "He's just yellow!"

"We'll squash you as flat as the Egyptian desert!"

"We'll pull off your horns and turn them into hieroglyphs!"

"We'll make you into a mummy!" And so on and so forth. But still the Golden Snail did not appear.

Then Queen of the Ants grew angry, thinking the Snail was trying to make her look foolish.

"We'll teach these snails a lesson!" she cried to her assembled army. "I hereby declare war on the Snails of Surbiton! Let's wipe them off the map!"

And then there was a great noise, as the army of Robber Ants ground their mandibles together to make a sound like all the knives of the world being sharpened at once. And they raised their voices in a great roar of anger.

"Forward, Ants! Destroy the Snails!" cried their Queen.

And so they advanced, and with every step they took, the ground shook and all the wild life of Surbiton trembled in their burrows and dens and hiding holes.

As they moved forward, however, they suddenly heard a voice, louder than the din they were making, and it said: "This is the Golden Snail of Surbiton speaking! I command you to lay down your weapons and halt your marching, before I am forced to destroy you all!"

The Robber Ants didn't know quite what to do, because the voice of the Golden Snail was so loud and so commanding. Some of them stopped and some of them went on, with the result that they all fell over each other and there was total confusion.

"Where are you, Golden Snail?" roared The Champion of the Robber Ants, whose name was Snag-Knees Rhino-Squasher the 3rd. "I will come and fight you face to face and put an end to all this nonsense!"

"I'm over here! To your right!" said the voice. "Come and get me!" and the army of Ants turned as one to see the Golden Snail of Surbiton sitting – as cool as a cucumber – on top of a huge mound of leaves and speaking through a megaphone.

Well of course, the army didn't hesitate! It charged at the Golden Snail. But the Golden Snail of Surbiton hardly gave them a glance. He was too busy munching on a leaf.

"Kill him!" screamed the Queen Ant.

"AAAAAARGGHHHH!" roared the Robber Ants!

"What's going on?" shouted the leading ants.

"Help!" cried the next row.

"Stop!" roared Snag-Knees Rhino-Squasher the 3rd.

"Stop!" cried another.

"Stop! Stop!" cried even more of the Robber Ants.

But it was too late! The Robber Ants at the back of the army couldn't hear, and couldn't stop anyway – they kept on pushing forward and falling over each other and nobody could stop even as they began to realize that the Golden Snail had set up his pile of leaves right in the middle of the Great Swamp of Surbiton! For, of course, a small snail can slide across the surface of a swamp, without even thinking about it. But not Giant Robber Ants the size of elephants!

Before you could say "Rameses!" the Blind Swamp Lizard was on the attack, and the Swamp Rats were gnawing through the Giant Robber Ants, and the Venomous Snakes and Poisonous Toads were churning up the mud of the swamp in their rush to get at them.

And that day the Vultures that circled above the Great Swamp of Surbiton had a feast the like of which they never had had before nor ever would have again.

"And that," said Great Grandfather Snail, "was how the Golden Snail of Surbiton rid the world of the Giant Robber Ants and made Surbiton the safe place it is today."

"But you still haven't explained why he was called the Golden Snail of Surbiton!" the little snails would chorus.

"Well," Grandfather Snail would reply, "it was because he lived in Surbiton."

"But why was he called 'Golden', Grandfather?"

"Ah! That was because he ate nothing but gold – he was just pretending to eat the leaves you see – and eating nothing but gold, of course, gave a golden hue to his shell. And in the night he would glow as if he were illuminated from within by his own daring and cleverness. He was the greatest snail that ever lived, and do you know what?"

"No, Grandfather," the little snails would say, although they knew perfectly well what was coming.

"His name was Arthur."

"But that's *your* name, Grandfather!" the little ones would chorus.

"Yes," Grandfather Snail would say. "It is…"

WONDERS OF THE ANIMAL KINGDOM

MONEY SALAMANDERS

These salamanders have acquired an extensive working knowledge of finance and are ready to advise anyone who is interested in investing large sums of money. However they are not trustworthy animals. If caught in some financial irregularity they will shed their tails, which will continue to wriggle for many minutes, distracting cheated investors and financial regulators, while the salamander hides itself in some tax haven.

THE FROG WHO
FOUND A FORTUNE

AN UNUSUALLY SENSIBLE FROG was hopping along under a hedge when he happened to spot something bright and sparkling in amongst the leaves and mud. He pulled it out, and gasped.

"If I didn't know that such a thing were impossible, I would say that this was nothing less than an extremely valuable and precious Diamond!" he said to himself.

He turned the jewel over and it glinted in the Spring sunshine with all the colours of the rainbow. It glittered and sparkled and somehow it took a remarkable hold on that unusually sensible frog's mind.

"I have no doubt," he said to himself, "that many hundreds of years ago, the King of England rode by this very hedgerow, and as he passed this Precious Diamond fell out of his crown, and rolled under this very hedge where I discovered it today.

"I must take it straight away to Buckingham Palace, where the Queen of England will be very glad to receive it. She will say: 'This Precious Diamond was the greatest jewel in the Crown of England. It has been missing for hundreds of years, and us kings and queens have had to wear the Crown of England back-to-front so that no one would notice it was missing. But now, you, O Frog, have brought the Precious Diamond back. I must knight you at once!'

"And Her Majesty will take out her sword, which she always carries by her side, and touch my shoulders with it and say: 'Arise, Sir Frog!'

"And she'll probably reward me beyond my wildest dreams. Who knows? She might even offer me a *whole* barrow-load of slugs! But I would say:

"Your Majesty! I could not possibly accept a whole barrow-load of slugs! Half a barrow-load would be more than sufficient!"

"But," Her Majesty will insist: "Sir Frog! Your modesty does you credit, but you have rendered the most noble and selfless service to me and to the people of England. No longer will their monarchs have to wear the Crown of England back-to-front! If my kingdom could supply three or even four barrow-loads of slugs, you should have them, for you so richly deserve them. Take the slugs and live happily ever after."

"And so she would order one of her servants to wheel the barrow-load of slugs back home for me. And then I would sell the slugs and become immensely wealthy. In fact I would become the richest frog who ever lived.

"I would build a huge mansion on that hill over there, with turrets and battlements and my Dear Lady Frog would look out of the window in the high tower and wave her handkerchief to me when I came home in the evening, after a day out selling slugs.

"But it may well be that such slugs as the Queen of England might pick out for her most favoured courtier would be the fattest and juiciest and most valuable slugs in existence, and after all she is giving me a *whole* barrow-load, so it might be that even building a huge mansion with turrets and battlements would not use up the money I should make from selling such slugs. So what should I do with the extra?

"I should invest it in a Slug Farm, where I would breed slugs. I would look after them so well that the slugs would flourish and increase in size and number so that I would become the greatest slug farmer on Earth!

"I would export vast shiploads of the Finest Slugs to South America, Africa, China and Australia. I would employ an army of book-keepers and managers and servants to help run the enterprise, and the money would keep pouring in so that eventually I would have to build an even bigger house with even more turrets and battlements, or else I should buy gowns and precious jewels for my Dear Lady Frog."

And the Frog sighed to himself with contentment, but then a shadow passed over his frog's face.

"There is, however, one snag," he thought. "I have no idea in which direction

Buckingham Palace lies! Is it this side of the hedge or the other side of the hedge? And should I follow the hedge to the East or follow it to the West? Or should I – perish the thought – leave the hedge entirely and venture out into the wide, wide world? Oh dear! This hedge is so nice and damp and shady, it would be a pity to leave it. It's hard to know what to do – particularly as I don't even know what Buckingham Palace looks like.

"And, in any case, how am I going to carry the Precious Diamond? It is so big that I'll be exhausted before I get to the end of the hedge whichever way I went."

Well, the more he thought about the problem of getting to Buckingham Palace, and how to carry the Precious Diamond, and what he would say to the footman who opened the door and demanded to know why a frog had rung the doorbell, and how on earth he'd manage to reach up to ring the doorbell in the first place, the more confused the poor Frog became, and the more confused he became, the more he couldn't think of anything else except his problem, and he failed to notice a Notorious Magpie, creeping up on him.

The first thing he knew was when the Notorious Magpie darted forward, snapped up the Precious Diamond in its beak and flew off with it – before the Frog could even croak: "Hey!"

The Frog watched as the Notorious Magpie flew up into the high branches of a tree and dropped the Precious Diamond into its nest, far away out of the Frog's reach.

The Frog blinked and said: "I'll not be going to Buckingham Palace after all! The Queen will never reward me with a *whole* barrow-load of the Best Slugs In The World, and I shall never build a huge mansion, nor sell a single slug, nor invest the money I make in a Slug Farm, and have to employ hundreds of people to export slugs around the world and take care of all that money I should make. Well! Thank goodness for that!"

And he hopped back under the lovely damp hedge and continued on his way.

He was, as I mentioned before, an unusually sensible frog.

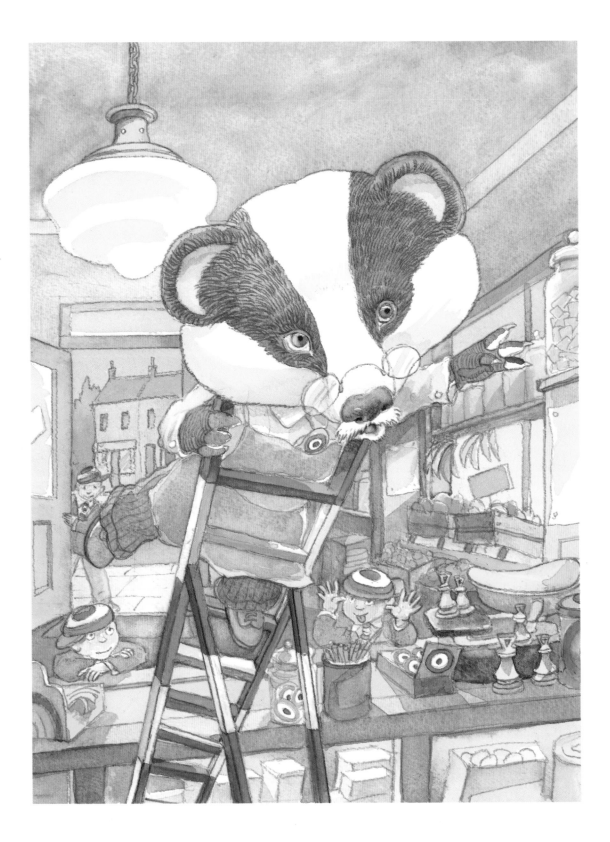

THE FLYING BADGER

THE BADGER, WHO KEPT OUR VILLAGE SHOP when I was a boy, was a grumpy sort of animal, and the shop had a very odd smell. When you walked in, Old Badger would emerge from the dimly-lit room behind the counter, and stand there watching you, as you tried to decide between a packet of sherbet with a liquorice straw or a gobstopper.

He would often snort, as if he were urging you to make up your mind, and shuffle his feet and scratch his elbows with his sharp claws. He always wore grey woollen gloves with the fingers cut off, so he could count the money.

Now why I'm telling you all this is because there was one kind of sweet we would always ask for even though we didn't really like them. Now you are probably thinking: "Why ask for a sweet that you don't like?" And that is a fair question.

The reason was this: whenever you asked for almond crunches a momentary look of terror would pass across Old Badger's face, and his paw would start to tremble. Then he would shut his eyes, take a deep breath, and say:

"You'll have to help me get them down."

Now Old Badger kept the almond crunches right up on the highest shelf. To get the jar he had to climb a stepladder, pull the jar off the shelf, and balance it on his fingertips. Then he would say in that quick, gruff way of his:

"Come on, Boy! Take the jar!"

He would stand there at the top of the stepladder, swaying dangerously and trying not to look down, and we would wait until it really looked as if he were going to fall, before we'd grab the jar of sweets.

Then we'd look anxious and say: "Are you all right, Mr. Badger?"

"Yes! Yes! Yes!" he'd reply crossly. "Of course I'm all right!"

And then he'd shut his eyes and climb down very slowly, until he was back on solid ground.

But here's the thing: he would always…*always*…forget to charge us for the almond crunches. So you see it didn't matter that we didn't like them, and they gave us a laugh at Old Badger's expense.

It was only much later, when I met the distinguished historian, Dame Polly Perrot, that I discovered what an amazing and extraordinary creature Old Badger really was.

"Old Badger was the bravest of the brave," Dame Polly said. "He was a revered figure and rightly so," and she told me the following story.

Before he ran the village shop, Old Badger had been a fighter pilot. He had flown Spitfires in the Second World War, being a member of RAF Badger Squadron. He flew over 149 'sorties' and shot down an uncounted number of enemy planes.

One particularly dark night, Badger Squadron was detailed to escort a bombing mission deep into enemy territory. Now badgers have superb night vision, and the Germans were baffled how we were able to fly and find the target no matter how black the night. But, of course, they didn't have any badgers on active service.

Well Old Badger was by then squadron leader, but most of the badgers under him were new to the game, and that sometimes caused problems.

"Our job is to see these bombers get to their target and safely home again," he told them. "You've got to stick with the bombers – even if it means passing up a chance to bag an enemy fighter!"

Well the young badgers grumbled a good deal about this.

"It's all right for Old Badger," they murmured. "He's shot down lots of jerries, but he's not giving us the chance!"

They set off after sunset, and climbed through the thick clouds, until they came out above them, and there was the Moon, bright as a new shilling.

Then all of a sudden, two squadrons of Messerschmitts came at them: one squadron from the east and the other from the west.

Old Badger kept his head.

"You bombers dive!" he radioed. "We'll keep jerry occupied!" And the bombers dived into the clouds below, where the enemy couldn't see them. Meanwhile Badger Squadron was attacking the enemy fighters.

Old Badger was first to score a direct hit, sending an enemy plane spiralling down, while the pilot scrambled out in his parachute and soon disappeared into the clouds below.

And soon the young badgers, with their superb night vision, were notching up hit after hit as well. Pretty soon the enemy decided it was too hot to stick around.

"There they go!" shouted Old Badger over the radio. "Well played, you young badgers!"

But the young badgers weren't listening. Their blood was up, and they simply couldn't stop themselves giving chase.

"Tally ho!" they all started shouting. "Let's get 'em!" And they were making so much noise, none of them heard Old Badger shouting:

"No! No! You've got to stay with the bombers!"

Off went the Spitfires of Badger Squadron, and Old Badger was left to escort the bombing mission all on his own.

"All clear!" he radioed to the bombers, and one by one they rose up out of the cloud below.

"Lost a few friends?" asked the leading bomber sympathetically.

"'Fraid so," Old Badger radioed back, for he didn't want to tell them that the young badgers had abandoned the mission.

They flew on into Germany itself. At length, they dived down below the cloud, and there were the German bomb factories spread out below them. Their mission was to drop their bombs on as many bomb factories as possible. And pretty soon, the British bombers found themselves engulfed in enemy fire.

Nonetheless, they dropped their bombs and quickly disappeared back up into the cloud.

Old Badger knew that the return journey was just as dangerous as the trip out, so he kept his eyes open for any sign of the enemy. And sure enough, another squadron of Messerschmitts descended on them from above.

"Dive!" he shouted to the bombers, as the enemy opened fire. The bomber pilots put their planes into a steep descent to take cover in the cloud below, but not before several

bullets had found their mark.

Old Badger, stayed up above the cloud and climbed even higher. Then he dived on first one Messerschmitt and then another. Two of them went down in flames, and Old Badger saw the parachutes of the pilots disappear into the cloud. Then another was coming straight for him and another was on his tail! Quick as a flash he dived again, and the two enemy planes collided in mid-air.

The last remaining Messerschmitt came down at Old Badger from out of the Moon. It started firing straight at him but he banked, so the bullets went under his wheel case. But, as luck would have it, one bullet caught the Spitfire slap-bang in the fuel tank, and the petrol started gushing out behind him.

Old Badger was done for, and he expected to be shot out of the sky at any moment. But the German pilot was a decent stick, who refused to shoot down a plane that was already a 'goner'.

Old Badger could see the German pilot giving him a salute as if to say: "You fought well, Old Badger! I'm sorry you won't have enough fuel to get you home!"

Then that gallant German turned his fighter around and headed off back to Germany – leaving Old Badger to run out of fuel and ditch in the cold North Sea.

But Old Badger wasn't thinking of his own plight. He was determined to see that the bombers all made it safely back to England, even if he didn't.

He radioed 'All Clear!' to the lead bomber, but there was no reply. Then a voice shouted: "The pilot's copped a bullet! He's alive but unconscious!"

"Can any of you fly the plane?" asked Old Badger.

"No," came the reply, "none of us have a clue."

"Can you pull the plane up out of the cloud?" he asked.

"I'll give it a try!" replied the Navigator.

So Old Badger told the Navigator what to do, and the rest of the bombers followed.

Now this is where Old Badger showed what a truly amazing and extraordinary creature he was.

"Fly straight ahead and keep absolutely level!" he told the Navigator of the lead bomber.

"Aye aye! Badger!" radioed back the Navigator.

Then Old Badger flew his doomed Spitfire twenty feet above the bomber, slid back the canopy of his cockpit and hauled himself out into the icy wind.

Can you guess what he did next? Yes! He jumped, falling through the cold night air from one plane to the other! Perhaps it was a foolhardy thing to do, but it was certainly the bravest act I've ever heard of. And do you know what? He was lucky. He landed fair and square on the nose of the bomber.

The Navigator pulled Old Badger in, but the Spitfire had now run out of fuel, and it began to drop. So Old badger threw himself at the controls and gave the bomber a boost of speed, so that the Spitfire dropped harmlessly behind its tail, and fell through the cloud to crash into black North Sea.

Well of course, the crews of the entire squadron of bombers burst into applause, and Old Badger flew that bomber safely back to England. By the time they landed, word had got about of Old Badger's amazing feat, and for many weeks after that Old Badger was the toast of the R.A.F.

But the strange thing was that, despite the glory, Old Badger seemed to lose his nerve after that. He never flew another mission, and when people asked him to tell the story he'd tell them to mind their own business.

So no wonder Old Badger turned pale when boys asked for the almond crunches, and no wonder we laughed at him when we saw he was afraid of heights.

But then none of us knew that Old Badger was one of the bravest of the brave.

THE FAKE ELK

The so-called "Fake Elk" is in fact a real elk that disguises itself as a plaster model and stands around, stock-still, at the back of cinemas. There it waits for some heart-breaking moment, or an exciting climax, and then it charges about the cinema, creating havoc with its loud bellowing and attacking the screen with its antlers. The result is that the audience's appreciation of the film is ruined.

Naturally it is in great demand during the Oscar season when unscrupulous film companies smuggle them into rival screenings.

THE ELEPHANT WHO HAD NO TROUSERS

SIR REGINALD ELEPHANT WAS A VERY RESPECTABLE ANIMAL, but it grieved him that he had no trousers.

"I must have a pair of trousers for the Queen's Visit!" he said. So he went to the Monkey to get a suit made. The Monkey measured him from the tip of his trunk to the tip of his tail, and then shook his head.

"I'm sorry, Sir Reginald," said the Monkey, "I simply don't have enough cloth to make you a suit."

"That's all right!" replied Sir Reginald. "It's only the trousers I'm really interested in. Just make me a pair of trousers."

"Alas!" said the Monkey. "I don't have enough cloth for even one trouser leg in your size."

"Bother!" said Sir Reginald Elephant, and he went along to the Goat who lived under the Cabbage Tree.

"Goat, old fellow!" said Sir Reginald. "I desperately need a pair of trousers for the Queen's Visit. Monkey hasn't got enough cloth to make even one trouser leg – so I wonder if you could let me have a bit of your wool?"

The Goat gave Sir Reginald a sour look, and tossed its head.

"It's not *wool*!" he exclaimed. "And I'm not an "old fellow"! I'm a young Angora Goat and my *fleece* is extremely expensive!"

"Terribly sorry, old chap!" said Sir Reginald Elephant. "Didn't mean to cause offence."

And he lumbered off, muttering to himself: "Bother!"

When he got to the river, there were some sheep standing in a field, so Sir Reginald leaned over the fence and called out:

"I say! I need a spot of wool for a pair of trousers for the Queen's Visit! Could you oblige?"

But the sheep shook their heads.

"All our wool belongs to the fa...aaa...aaa...aaarmer," they said. "We ca...aaa...aaa...aaan't just give it away to the first e-e-e-e-elephant who aaa...aaa...aaasks!"

Sir Reginald Elephant went and stood in the shade of a Baobab Tree, for the sun was getting rather warm, and then he said "Bother!" again.

"What's up, mate?" asked a Weaver Ant who was scurrying along one of the branches of the Baobab Tree.

"I need a pair of trousers for the Queen's Visit," explained Sir Reginald. "But there just isn't enough cloth to make 'em. And nobody seems to be able to help."

"Maybe I can, old sport!" said the ant.

"That's very kind of you," replied Sir Reginald, "but when I look at your size and the striking absence of any wool, or even fleece, on your back, I very much doubt it."

"Brother Elephant," said the Weaver Ant, "don't worry your noddle about that!"

And before Sir Reginald could wave his trunk, there were half a million ants swarming down the branch and over his legs.

"I say! That tickles!" exclaimed Sir Reginald Elephant, and if you've ever had half a million ants crawling over your legs, you'd know exactly what he meant.

"Hold still, Brother Elephant!" cried the Weaver Ant. "My mates are just measuring you up!"

And sure enough, before Sir Reginald had a chance to blow his trunk, those half a million ants had scurried off his legs and were all over the Baobab Tree.

"What's going on?" cried Sir Reginald Elephant, as the ants pulled leaf after leaf off the Baobab and then scurried back to him

"Hold still, Brother Elephant!" shouted the Weaver Ant as the other ants swarmed up the Elephant's tail and over his back legs, pulling the leaves with them. And before Sir Reginald had a chance to adjust his spectacles, those ants had started to sew the leaves together – which is, after all, what Weaver Ants do.

Chains of ants held the leaves in place, while the others sewed and knitted, until they'd made a whole pair of trousers out of leaves, that fitted Sir Reginald Elephant just as if they had been made for him – which of course they had.

When the Weaver Ants had finished, Sir Reginald did a little twirl around to show his new trousers off, and the ants all stood back and admired their own handiwork.

"Green trousers!" exclaimed Sir Reginald. "Just the job! Whoopeee! Is there anything I can do for you ants?"

"Just try not to tread on us in future," said the Weaver Ant.

"Absolutely!" cried Sir Reginald, and, taking great care where he put his feet, he went off to wait for the Queen's Visit.

Well the Queen didn't visit that week, nor the week after, nor the week after that, and Sir Reginald began to think she would never come. However, the rains passed and the dry season came, and finally the word got around the jungle that the Queen was on her way.

Now the Boabab tree loses its leaves in the dry season, and so it was that Sir Reginald's trousers turned a beautiful shade of gold.

"My word!" exclaimed Sir Reginald. "I bet those Weaver Ants didn't realize what a valuable pair of trousers they'd given me! Imagine! I'll be wearing golden trousers when I meet the Queen! I wouldn't be surprised if she says: 'Kneel, Sir Reginald! You are too magnificent an elephant to remain a mere knight! Arise, Lord Reginald of The Golden Trousers!' That's what she'll say!" And he started to parade around the jungle, showing off his golden trousers to every animal who cared to look.

Eventually the great morning came, and Sir Reginald was in a regular tizz. He hadn't slept a wink all night, and now, as he stood in a prominent position where the Queen would be sure to notice him, he found himself nodding off. But he tried to pull himself together.

"It would be too dreadful for words if I were to miss Her Majesty's visit because I was asleep," he kept telling himself, and forcing his eyes to stay open.

He stood there through the dawn rush for the waterhole. He stood there as the sun rose higher, and the scrub began to crackle as if it were cooking in the heat, though really it was the sound of myriads of insects and out-of-sight creatures. He stood there till noon, with the sun beating down, until the heat became as real and as solid as another elephant standing by his side.

He stood there, with his eyelids closing and closing, ready for the moment when Her Majesty should deign to notice him in his golden trousers. And eventually he couldn't help himself: Sir Reginald Elephant nodded off.

The littlest monkeys started pulling faces at him and climbing up his trunk. But their mothers shook their heads.

"Poor Sir Reginald," they said.

"And he went to such trouble to find a pair of trousers."

"And such smart trousers they are…"

But they didn't say anything more, because Sir Reginald had begin to snore, and the monkey mothers couldn't hear what each other was saying.

At that moment, all the animals (apart from Sir Reginald Elephant of course) saw a cloud of dust on the horizon, that seemed to be coming nearer and nearer.

"It's the royal party," announced one of the lions, who had ambitions to become a Palace Correspondent.

And sure enough, just under Sir Reginald's vociferous snoring they could hear the sound of several motor cars bouncing over the hot and dusty plain.

"It looks like Her Majesty is wearing a safari hat instead of her usual crown," said the lion sounding a trifle disappointed.

However the lions all arranged themselves in a typical pose that they thought would impress Her Majesty, with Father Lion standing proudly looking into the distance and Mother Lion lying contentedly by his side and the cubs playing cutely at their feet.

Even the leopards had got themselves organized by the time the Royal party drew up to them. The leopards were prowling about looking distinctly irritated, which is what any visitor to the wilds of Africa expects leopards to look like.

As the dust from the car wheels subsided, various men leapt out of the vehicles and one of them rushed to the leading Land Rover and opened the door. The Queen climbed out

and looked around her, as the Ranger pointed out the lions in their typical pose and warned Her Majesty not to try and feed the leopards.

"One can assure you that one has absolutely no intention of trying to feed those beasts – they look particularly dangerous," replied Her Majesty.

"As indeed they are," said the Ranger. Then under his breath he muttered to the leopards: "Well done boys."

"But what is that dreadful noise, Ranger?" asked the Queen. "It sounds like the Martians attacking in *The War of the Worlds*."

"I am afraid it is the elephant who has fallen asleep," replied the Ranger.

"Then pray wake him up at once!" commanded the Queen. "I can hardly hear myself think!"

So the Ranger nodded to the drivers of the Land Rovers and they all hit their horns at once, and the horns made such a noise it woke Sir Reginald Elephant from his deep sleep.

Now Sir Reginald had been having a dream in which the entire Cheltenham Ladies College had been visiting him for tea, and all the Ladies had been particularly admiring of his golden trousers. But some leopards happened to be passing by and they started jeering and making rude noises that got louder and louder until it sounded like lots of car horns blaring at once. Whereupon Sir Reginald woke up feeling very indignant.

"Shut up!" he yelled at the Royal party. "You rude, ill-bred creatures! And that goes for you too!" He said to their leader, who was wearing a safari hat.

Well there was a silence in which you might hear a pin drop.

And then Sir Reginald began to realize where he was, and that the leopards were actually the Royal Party and the lady in the safari hat was none other than Her Majesty the Queen of England, herself!

Sir Reginald Elephant wished he could sink into the ground and disappear, but since he couldn't do that, he decided to make a run for it. Now his golden trousers were only golden, of course, because the leaves had died, and so when he decided to make a run for it he span round and shook the leaves so violently that they began to fall. As they fell around his feet, with the Queen of England looking on, Sir Reginald tried desperately to catch them, and that was when he made his big mistake.

When you think of the construction of an elephant, and the way it stands on four legs, it's obvious what will happen if it tries to pull up its trousers. And that is indeed what happened. Sir Reginald fell flat on his face in front of the Queen! His chin hit the ground and his trunk flailed out across the dry earth, sending up all the dust that had just settled in dense cloud, immediately engulfing Her Majesty.

When the dust settled, a lot of it had settled *on* the Queen of England. She stood there, like a stone statue, along with her flunkies and butlers and personal assistants all standing there as if they had been turned to stone.

Sir Reginald swallowed once. Then twice. Then he blinked. Then he scrambled to his feet, and ran. He ran as fast as he could and as far away as possible, leaving his trousers lying on the ground in front of the Queen and her entourage.

And the Queen's flunkies and butlers and personal assistants looked at her with open mouths, expecting her to order the elephant to be caught and destroyed or perhaps sent to some prison for rogue elephants if she were feeling particularly merciful. But she didn't.

Instead she burst into laughter and, of course, that is also what the flunkies and butlers and personal assistants did too. The Ranger and the trackers and the drivers of the Land Rovers joined in, and they all started laughing and laughing and laughing.

And even though Sir Reginald had disappeared into the deepest part of the jungle, that laughter followed him all the way home.

Some time later, the Monkey approached Sir Reginald Elephant, and said:

"Sir Reginald, I am so sorry I could not oblige you with a pair trousers the other week. However, I am happy to be able to tell you I have now secured enough cloth to make you the full suit. I await your instructions."

Sir Reginald turned to the Monkey Tailor. "My dear sir," he said. "I left my trousers with the Queen of England. I shall never wear another pair, until she sees fit to return them."

And he gave the Monkey a polite nod, and went on his way.

THE SKUNK & THE BEAR

A LITTLE SKUNK ONCE FELL IN LOVE WITH A BEAR. "You are the most handsome, the bravest and most charming creature in the whole forest," she told him. "I love your rough fur coat, your rough voice, and your rough ways. But I see you are also a thoughtful bear, for I have often observed you sitting and thinking. I could imagine no greater happiness than to have my life bound up with yours."

But Bear didn't reply, for he was fast asleep. Perhaps Little Skunk would never have dared tell him all those things if he'd been awake.

Little Skunk would wait for Bear to come out of his cave, and she would watch him waking up and stretching. She loved the way he blinked in the sunlight. She loved the way he rose up on his great hind legs to sniff the breeze and the way he rubbed his snout with his strong fore paws. She loved the way his fur glistened and shook as he came down on all fours and loped off through the trees.

Her friends told Little Skunk to forget about Bear. "Bears and skunks can't mix," they said. "It's ridiculous! What could you ever do for a bear? And what could a bear ever do for you?"

But it didn't make any difference. Little Skunk still loved his great brown eyes and his pink tongue.

Then one day something terrible happened. Some men entered the forest and laid a trap for Bear.

Now Bear was a wary creature, and that morning when he stood up on his hind legs and sniffed the breeze, he could smell that men had been in the forest, so he was extra watchful. And that was how, peering around, he caught sight of Little Skunk as she gazed at him through the trees.

It so happens that bears are particularly disgusted by the dreadful scent that skunks produce, so as soon as Bear saw Little Skunk, he turned away and hurried off into the forest in the opposite direction.

Little Skunk saw how Bear had hurried to avoid her, and she felt ashamed.

"If only I weren't a skunk!" she exclaimed to herself. "Our only gift is the gift of stinking. No wonder the other creatures of the forest look down on us. No wonder Bear shuns me!"

And Little Skunk felt a tear welling up in her eye, but she stamped her foot.

"We can none of us help what we are born as!" she said. "And since I've been born a skunk, it's wrong to be ashamed of it. I'm going to tell Bear what I feel for him. Why shouldn't I?"

And she started to run after Bear as fast as she could.

Now Bear heard Little Skunk running after him, and he said to himself: "Skunks don't normally run after us bears. They are usually so afraid of us that, as soon as they see us, they immediately produce their dreadful stink, that makes us bears feel ill. What's more if we get that foul-smelling scent on our skins it'll itch like mad, and if we get it in our eyes it can blind us. And for any creature of the forest to be blind even for a short while can be a death sentence. But the worst – the very worst – thing about skunks' smell is that if I ever got it on my beautiful shiny fur, I could never clean it off and I would stink forever!"

No wonder that Bear, when he found himself pursued by Little Skunk, ran headlong through the forest, and no wonder he failed to see the place where the leaves had been disturbed by the Trappers' feet.

Little Skunk did not see the trap spring, but she heard the jump of the metal, and she heard Bear's howl of pain and surprise, as the jaws of the trap clamped around his hind leg. Little Skunk burst into the clearing where Bear was caught. She saw his leg covered in blood, with the great iron trap holding him down. She saw the wide-eyed fear on Bear's face and equally she saw the look of disgust as his eye fell upon her.

Little Skunk's first thought was to try and get Bear free, but Bear was filled with mortal fear, and he growled and bared his teeth and tried to claw Little Skunk as she approached the trap.

"Don't worry, Bear! I won't release my stink on you. I've come to rescue you, Bear, because all this time I've been in love with your power and strength, the great beauty of your snout and ears, and the glorious lustre of your fur. I love you, Bear."

That's what Little Skunk wanted to say, but she never got the chance, because there was suddenly the sound of men shouting and crashing through the undergrowth as the Trappers burst into the clearing to claim their prize.

"It's a big brown!" exclaimed one of the Trappers, and he raised his gun. There was a bang, and Little Skunk fled – but only till she was hidden in the undergrowth. Then she turned to see what had happened.

The Trappers were standing in the clearing looking intently at Bear. Bear himself was still standing on all fours, with his hind leg caught in that dreadful trap, but he was swaying from side to side, and now suddenly he crumpled into a heap on the ground. Little Skunk watched as the men swarmed around the fallen Bear. Next moment she saw the men kick Bear's lifeless body, and laugh as they lifted up his limp paw and let it drop. Suddenly Little Skunk was seized by a violent anger. Who did these men think they were to treat Bear like that?

As the Trappers prised open the trap to free Bear's leg, a wild plan entered Little Skunk's head, and before she had even thought it through, she found herself racing back through the bushes and leaping into the clearing right into the middle of those men. The Trappers were so intent on what they were doing to Bear that they didn't notice her for the moment. But then one of them suddenly yelled:

"Look out! Skunk!"

The men turned, and on seeing Little Skunk, they scrambled to get away. In their panic, two of them collided with one another and fell over in a heap, while the other two dived into the undergrowth without thinking. But they were too late! Little Skunk turned her back on them and shot her scent with deadly accuracy – hitting one of them from six feet away. Then she aimed again, and this time sent her spray twelve feet through the air and hit another man on the back as he struggled through the undergrowth. And still she hadn't finished. With one last effort, she shot yet another spray of scent fifteen feet through the air and hit both the men who had fallen over each other.

But Little Skunk still hadn't finished. She was so angry that she just turned right around and chased after those men. One of them glanced over his shoulder and shouted:

"That crazy skunk! It's coming after us! Look out!"

And they ran as if their lives depended on it.

Meanwhile back in the clearing, Bear began to groan. The Trappers had stunned him with a tranquilizer dart, but that wasn't strong enough to withstand the powerful scent of skunk. One load of scent might have been enough to bring Bear to his senses, but Little Skunk had released no less than three times the normal amount, and the stink was now so powerful that Bear started coughing and choking and his eyes smarted and he regained his senses enough to struggle to his feet and try to stagger as far away from that stench as his wounded leg would let him.

By the time Little Skunk got back to the clearing, Bear had disappeared, but she could see a trail of blood leading from the cruel jaws of the trap, across the clearing and into the forest, so she began to follow it with beating heart.

Over tree stumps, through broken undergrowth, she could see where Bear had blundered on his way, but the trail seemed to be going around in circles, and then suddenly she saw a great bulk lying beside a fallen tree.

For the first time, Little Skunk found herself feeling afraid of Bear. "After all," she told herself, "he doesn't know I rescued him from the Trappers."

Nonetheless, Little Skunk jumped up onto the fallen tree and shouted: "Bear! Bear! Wake up! You must get back to your cave before the Trappers return!"

Bear managed to open one eye and gasp: "Why are you so concerned about me, Little Skunk? What have I ever done for you?"

Should Little Skunk tell him she'd chased off the Trappers? Should she tell him she loved him?

But before she could speak another voice said:

"Now this is curious: Little Skunk deep in conversation with Bear. Well, well! What on earth is the forest coming to?"

Little Skunk and Bear looked round to see Wolf standing in the clearing gazing thoughtfully at them.

"Bears usually avoid Skunks as if they had the plague," went on Wolf. "What could have brought about this sweet little friendship I wonder?"

"Stay away from me!" exclaimed Little Skunk, stamping the ground and hissing at Wolf. "Or else I'll spray you and you'll never wash the stink off your fine fur!"

And with that she turned her back on Wolf to spray him.

Now I have to tell that a skunks only carry a limited amount of their terrible stink, which is why they are normally reluctant to use it.

But Little Skunk had been so concerned about Bear and so angry with the Trappers, that she had used up all her stink and now she had none left.

"Well?" said Wolf. "If you're going to spray me and make my fur stink forever, go ahead! I'm waiting!"

Now whether wily Wolf had seen everything that had happened or not, I don't know, but somehow he knew that Little Skunk was helpless, and somehow Little Skunk knew that he knew. So there was only one thing she could do, and she did it. She turned and ran.

She ran so fast through the undergrowth that the branches whipped at her face and the thorns tore through her fur. But she didn't even notice them. She ran faster than she had ever done in her life.

Wolf, however, was quicker. His long legs vaulted him over logs and fallen branches and in no time he was upon Little Skunk.

He seized her by the tail, and she turned and scratched him on the nose. But he no more noticed that than Little Skunk had noticed the thorns; all he could think about was his dinner. Wolf tossed Little Skunk through the air, and the sound of her head cracking against the ground gave Wolf a nice, cosy feeling that he would be soon be eating.

Little Skunk, however, leapt to her feet, her head still spinning, and turned to bare her teeth at Wolf, but she was facing the wrong way. A cold thrill went through her as she felt Wolf's teeth on the back of her neck, and his hot wolf's breath ruffle her fur!

Little Skunk knew that her last moment had come. She hissed and spat but she had no scent to drive Wolf back. Her last thought was:

"I never told Bear I loved him. He will never know it was me who saved him from the Trappers."

And she shut her eyes and waited for Wolf to bite.

But something happened. Wolf did not bite her. Instead it was Wolf's turn to find himself thrown across the forest until he hit a tree, and slid down the trunk into a bush of brambles.

Little Skunk looked round to see Bear gazing down on her.

"Little Skunk," said Bear. "Do you know where my cave is?"

"Yes," said Little Skunk.

"Then take me to it," said Bear. "I'm so bemuddled I don't know whether I'm coming or going."

Little Skunk thought she had never been happier, as she led Bear back to his cave. Bear was swaying as he limped behind her, and he kept bumping into trees and overhanging branches, so Little Skunk led him along the wider paths that she would normally have avoided: the paths of the bear, the tiger and the leopard.

When they arrived back at the cave, Bear lumbered in and without saying a word he keeled over, unconscious.

Little Skunk looked at Bear lying there. Would he remember her when he woke up? Would he ever know that she had rescued him from the Trappers? That she had guided him safely home? Would she ever get the chance to speak to him again?

Little Skunk turned and crept out of the cave. The sun was setting and the sky was as red as the trail of Bear's blood. The sounds of the forest's night creatures filled her ears, and then she heard another sound – a soft sound like a gentle rumble of thunder. It came from inside the cave.

"Thank you, Little Skunk," said the voice.

After that, Little Skunk often visited Bear, and although they never said very much to each other, Bear never tried to avoid her. There they would sit together outside the cave, an odd couple, watching the sun go down.

And whenever her friends scolded her and told her to forget about Bear and said: "It's ridiculous! What could you ever do for a bear? And what could a bear ever do for you?" Little Skunk would smile to herself and think:

"We could save each other's lives."

WONDERS OF THE ANIMAL KINGDOM

BENDY GIRAFFES

These giraffes can be bent in all sorts of shapes to make delightful Christmas gifts. A simple 896 page booklet gives detailed instructions on how to bend your giraffe into a whole range of useful household objects, such as: a four poster bed, a genuine antique bookcase, a chiming grandfather clock or even a simple bucket.

The last 60 pages contain simple easy-to-follow instructions on how to bend your giraffe into a surface-to-air missile system, complete with depleted uranium warheads, suitable for use in the Third World.

JACK THE RABBIT

JACK THE RABBIT LIVES IN a deluxe warren which is surrounded by a big park, full of trees and lawns and marble statues. Across the park stands a cottage in which Lord and Lady Bigwig's Gamekeeper is residing, on account of which Jack the Rabbit has been warned to keep away from the cottage lest he end up in a rabbit pie. But, since nobody has explained to him exactly what a rabbit pie is, he takes no notice, and lopes around the cottage all the time.

Well, one day Jack the Rabbit is loping past the dustbins outside the cottage, when who does he find himself nose-to-nose with but Old Mr. Fox himself!

Jack the Rabbit jumps right out of his skin and disappears around the corner so fast his tail only catches up with him moments later. Then Jack the Rabbit hides and waits for Old Mr. Fox to go on his way.

But Old Mr. Fox doesn't go on his way. And Jack the Rabbit waits and waits, and doesn't see snout nor tail of Old Mr. Fox.

Now it is a well-known fact that Jack the Rabbit is a cool customer, who doesn't take fright as easily as most rabbits do. In fact he has a reputation for having nerves of steel. Another thing for which he has a considerable reputation is his insatiable curiosity.

So after some time Jack the Rabbit thinks to himself: "You know there was something odd about Old Mr. Fox just now." And then he thinks to himself: "Maybe I should go and take another look at him."

So Jack the Rabbit does something which I don't think any other rabbit would have done in the circumstances, he lopes back round the corner to take another look at Old Mr. Fox.

And there he is: lying exactly where he was, which, when you consider how much business Old Mr. Fox has to get through in a night, takes some explaining.

"Hey! Old Mr. Fox!" shouts Jack the Rabbit. "Aren't you well or something?"

Well Old Mr. Fox doesn't say nothing. He just lies there with a glassy look in his eyes, perfectly still.

"What's the matter?" says Jack the Rabbit. "Fox got your tongue?" And Jack the Rabbit thinks that's so funny he does a little dance around. Then he hops right up to Old Mr. Fox and stretches out his hind leg and *touche*s him!

Well Old Mr. Fox just lies there with this glassy look in his eyes. And the next minute Jack the Rabbit kicks Old Mr. Fox on the snout and Old Mr. Fox doesn't do nothing. He just lies there as Jack the Rabbit kicks him again and again.

Now I have to tell you something you may find hard to believe, but all the same it's true. Many years ago a lot of elegant ladies thought they looked even more elegant if they hung a dead fox around their necks – complete with legs and tail and head. That's what the Gamekeeper's wife thought anyway, and she'd worn her fox fur on several occasions.

But fashions change, and it is the Gamekeeper's wife's fox fur, sticking out of the dustbin, that Jack the Rabbit comes nose-to-nose with when he's loping round the cottage on this very morning.

"Ah ha!" cries Jack the Rabbit. "Take that, Old Mr. Fox! You're not so clever now are you? Ho ho! I bet not many rabbits have ever kicked a fox!"

And while he's busy kicking Old Mr. Fox on the snout, Jack the Rabbit suddenly gets the Big Idea. It is the most super-sensational-extraordinary idea that any rabbit has ever had, *ever*.

"You're crazy!" says Bugsy Two Ears, when he hears what Jack the Rabbit is intending to do. And Bugsy Two Ears is a rabbit whose opinion is highly valued by rabbits who want to be considered worth their lettuce in the warren.

What's more, Louis the Loper, who happens to be a personal best friend of Jack the Rabbit, gets pretty excited when he hears of Jack's Big Idea.

"I am never hearing of such a lousy idea since Joey the Buck tried to date a lawn mower!" he exclaims, and emphasises his point by kicking Jack the Rabbit on his white tail.

But Jack the Rabbit is not to be put off, and the very next evening, he dresses himself up in that old, unfashionable fox fur, and he sets out to put his Big Idea into practice.

As he makes his way through the burrow, there are quite a number of rabbits who naturally jump out of their skins, rabbits being generally of a nervous disposition. In fact, there are several who yell out: "Arghh! It's Old Mr. Fox come to get us!" and fall over like skittles in an alley.

But Jack the Rabbit just grins and lopes off to the edge of the dark forest, still wearing the old fox fur draped over him. There he sits for some time, washing his ears, until he hears a certain noise. Now this noise is the sort of noise that would have any other rabbit racing back to the burrow, but Jack the Rabbit stays put right where he is. And pretty soon who should appear but Old Mrs. Fox and her two cubs.

She stops dead, when she spots Jack the Rabbit, and then stands there, glaring at him across the little clearing.

Well Jack the Rabbit is naturally a little excited at this moment, and his heart is thumping away like it's going for a world record. He can see Old Mrs. Fox's teeth behind the black line of her lips. What's more he can feel the old fox fur slipping off his back, and any minute now his rabbit ears are going to pop up like targets in a shooting gallery. But before any of this happens, Old Mrs Fox turns her back on Jack the Rabbit, and cuffs her cubs that are scampering around her feet like a couple of furry yo-yos.

Jack the Rabbit adjusts his disguise and waits to see what will happen next. Well what happens next is that one of the furry yo-yos scampers across the glade and right up to Jack the Rabbit. Now I'm not saying that Jack the Rabbit doesn't have a split second when he wishes he were back safe in his burrow, but split seconds tend to come and go, and that's exactly what this split second does. Before Jack the Rabbit realizes what he is doing, he cuffs the furry yo-yo so it rolls over like a ball and then comes back for more.

Next minute, the other furry yo-yo runs over to join in the fun, and Old Mrs. Fox just sits there watching Jack-the-Rabbit romping with her cubs as if he were their favourite uncle.

Eventually, however, she gets up and calls her cubs, and they scuttle across pulling Jack the Rabbit with them, like he was one of the pack, and they all four slink off over the hill and disappear.

Pretty soon Jack the Rabbit finds himself standing with Old Mrs. Fox and her two cubs outside the hen house at Holly farm. The cubs turn to watch their mother as Old Mrs. Fox gives a sharp intake of breath, that gets Jack the Rabbit wondering what she's seen. Then he sees it. Someone has forgotten to shut the door to the hen house. And it is indeed a well-known fact that when someone leaves the door to a hen house open, it is an invitation to any fox to enter and get acquainted with the inhabitants of that particular hen house.

The only thing standing in the way of Old Mrs. Fox's getting better acquainted with the inhabitants of the hen house at Holly Farm is the wire netting fence around the hen run. It seems that Farmer Lebowski has done a pretty thorough job of making the wire-netting fence fox-proof. But when you have such an experienced operator as Old Mrs. Fox, there is never going to be any wire-netting fence that is entirely fox-proof – especially when someone has forgotten to shut the door to the hen house!

Old Mrs. Fox sniffs the wire-netting fence up and down a good few number of times, and then she starts digging. Jack the Rabbit and the cubs watch as Old Mrs. Fox squeezes under the wire-netting fence and bounds across the hen-run up the plank and into the hen house of Holly Farm.

Well it doesn't take two seconds for Old Mrs. Fox to start getting better acquainted with those chickens, and pretty soon there is plenty of clucking and a lot of squawking, and the old hen house at Holly Farm shakes and rattles as if it's in the middle of an earthquake. The next minute hens are flying out of the hen house at Holly Farm screeching and making enough noise to awaken the dead or even (which is more to the point) Farmer Lebowski and his wife.

Old Mrs. Fox suddenly appears with the neck of the fattest of all the chickens firmly clamped in her jaws. She makes a bee-line for the place where she dug under the wire-netting fence, but as she does so the lights go on in Holly Farm, and the kitchen door is flung open as old Farmer Lebowski and his wife come running out.

Old Mrs. Fox dives for the hole under the wire-netting fence, but she can't get through on account of the chicken she has clamped in her jaws being such a big fat one. She tries this way and that but it's no use. In the meantime the shouting from the farmhouse is getting nearer and suddenly there is a flash and a bang and something whizzes past Jack the Rabbit's left ear.

Well Old Mrs. Fox must have lost her appetite at that moment, for she lets go of the chicken and scrambles through the hole she'd dug and out the other side. There is another flash and another thing whizzes over Jack the Rabbit's ears.

"Run!" hisses Old Mrs. Fox. And that's what Jack the Rabbit and the two cubs do, as Old Mrs. Fox heads straight back to the dark forest, where she has her den.

And now, as they dash through the undergrowth, a new idea occurs to Jack the Rabbit. And this idea is so extraordinary – so against every rabbit's instinct – that I don't think I would have believed it, if I did not have this information from a most reliable source. Jack the Rabbit follows Old Mrs. Fox back to her den, and when she dodges down the hole between the roots of an old oak tree, Jack the Rabbit follows right after her! Yes! Jack the Rabbit actually does something that no other rabbit has ever done in the whole history of rabbits: he enters a fox's den of his own free will!

When Jack the Rabbit actually finds himself in the tunnel at the entrance to the fox's den, he half thinks about turning right around and running back to his own warren. But he's so curious, he just has to carry on down, deeper and deeper into the fox's den, where the smell of fox is so strong that his knees turn wobbly and he can't think straight. So he holds his breath, and pretty soon he finds himself sitting amongst the cubs, while Old Mrs. Fox is lying panting by his side.

Jack the Rabbit can see that Old Mrs. Fox is greatly relieved to be back in her den. "What d'you know?" he says to himself. "It seems that foxes get frightened just the same as us rabbits!"

But before he has a chance to think any more about this surprising observation, he hears someone at the entrance to the den.

And suddenly Jack the Rabbit remembers that he's just a rabbit disguised as a fox, and that rabbits have as much business being inside a fox's den as a fly has up an alligator's nose. So Jack the Rabbit takes a hop, step and a jump up the tunnel, where he can see a snout poking into the entrance to the den. His blood turns cold as he realizes it's Old Mr. Fox – the *real* Old Mr. Fox – not just some old fox fur that some elegant lady has thrown on the garbage heap on account of it being no longer the fashion.

So Jack the Rabbit sprints back down the tunnel, and hides behind the fox cubs. But his heart is jumping so hard it could win the Olympic pole vault on its own *and* without a pole. Any second he expects Old Mr. Fox to leap into the den, teeth bared and those jaws wide open to bite off his head.

But that is not what happens.

Old Mr. Fox takes his time entering the den, and, when he does, he sidles in curiously slowly and crouches down beside his good lady wife. But he never once takes his eyes off Jack the Rabbit hiding under his old fox-fur. And Jack the Rabbit can feel Old Mr. Fox's eyes boring into him, and he's just about to give himself up, when Old Mr. Fox speaks.

"So," says Old Mr. Fox, "I see we have a new cub."

Old Mrs. Fox nods.

"He seems a promising youngster," says Old Mr. Fox. "I'll take him hunting with me."

"And that's what he did!" says Jack the Rabbit to his admiring relatives and friends when he returns to the warren. "We caught a field mouse in the railway embankment!"

"We?" queries Bugsy Two Ears, for he has never, ever heard of a rabbit catching a field mouse.

"Yes," replies Jack the Rabbit. "I helped to stop it running away. But Old Mr. Fox he didn't eat it. We hid it in a secret place that only he and I know."

"Why did you do that?" asks Lenny Big Foot.

"Because foxes have small stomachs," says Jack the Rabbit, "Which is why they are hiding bits of food so they can always find a snack should they get hungry. After that we went to the Council Tip where we dug up an old chicken carcass."

"Yeurrrrgh!" remarks Louis the Loper.

"Tomorrow, Old Mr. Fox is showing me how to catch chickens."

The next night, Jack the Rabbit puts on his old fox-fur and hops off to the edge of the dark forest to wait for Old Mr. Fox. But Old Mr. Fox doesn't show.

Jack the Rabbit sits there and nibbles a bit of grass and washes his ears until they get sore.

"Huh!" says Jack the Rabbit. "If Old Mr. Fox isn't going to teach me how to catch chickens, I'll just teach myself. I can catch a stupid chicken if I want to!"

And off lopes Jack the Rabbit to the hen house at Holly Farm. But it seems that Farmer Lebowski has taken great care to make sure the door to the hen house is shut and, what's more, that no fox is going to dig under the wire-netting fence. But Jack the Rabbit by now is not only *dressed* like a fox, he's actually starting to *think* like a fox.

He goes right up to the hen house and starts looking for a hole that he could just squeeze through.

"They won't be leaving a hole big enough for a fox to get in, but I'm a lot smaller than a fox..."

And as he is saying these very words, he finds himself staring at a small chink in the hen house, and through that small chink, Jack the Rabbit can see a beady eye blinking at him.

"Warrr!" yells Jack the Rabbit, and he pulls a horrible face and the chicken, to whom the beady eye belongs, squawks with fright, which naturally sets off all the other chickens in the hen house. And soon there is enough squawking and clucking to wake old Farmer Lebowski even if he were sleeping the sleep of the dead.

But Jack the Rabbit isn't thinking about such things right now, and he squeezes himself through the chink. It's such a tight fit that the old fox fur gets pulled right off his back.

But Jack the Rabbit is so excited he doesn't even notice, and soon he's racing up and down that hen house trying to catch one of those chickens.

And those chickens are squawking and beating their wings so fast there are more feathers in the air than air. And Jack the Rabbit is right there in the middle of all that hullabaloo trying to get his teeth around a chicken's neck – just like he'd seen Old Mrs. Fox do.

But something is wrong.

Jack the Rabbit suddenly realizes that those chickens aren't squawking with fright any more, they're angry! And what's more they are not flying away from him, those chickens are flying straight at him! And he also realizes that they are pecking him with their sharp beaks and scratching him with their sharp claws, and pretty soon Jack the Rabbit begins to think that chickens are not so stupid after all, and that if he could just get out of that hen house, he'll be a lot more respectful of chickens in the future.

Now this is the precise moment when Farmer Lebowski flings open the door of the hen house, yelling:

"Caught you red-handed! You no good fox!"

And Mrs. Lebowski shines her lamp into the hen house and it lights up Jack the Rabbit, who is himself looking more like a chicken and, what's more, one that is ready for the oven, on account of having most of his fur pecked off. Well Jack the Rabbit just falls over like he was dead, and Farmer Lebowski turns to his wife and says:

"Well don't that beat anything? A rabbit making out like he's a fox?"

"I wouldn't have believed it, if I hadn't seen it with my own two eyes!" testifies Mrs. Lebowski.

Then old Farmer Lebowski picks Jack the Rabbit up by his ears and stuffs him into his pocket.

"Looks like we'll be having ourselves a rabbit pie, Mrs. Lebowski," says Farmer Lebowski to his wife.

"Better'n fox pie, Mr. Lebowski," replies his wife.

Well Jack the Rabbit still doesn't know what a 'rabbit pie' is, but he doesn't intend to find out, so he keeps on pretending to be dead, until Farmer Lebowski and his wife are out of the hen run and halfway back towards the house. Then suddenly Jack the Rabbit leaps out of Farmer Lebowski's pocket and races off into the night as fast as his legs can carry him.

"Well I'm blowed!" says Farmer Lebowski.

"Seems to me," says Mrs. Lebowski, "that that there rabbit is about as crafty as a fox!"

Jack the Rabbit makes it back to the warren, and Bugsy Two Ears, Lenny Big Feet and Louis the Loper do not stop laughing for several weeks on account of Jack the Rabbit looking so like a plucked chicken. But Jack the Rabbit does not pay any notice to them. And to anyone who asks him what has happened to his fur he replies:

"Foxes are foxes and rabbits are rabbits and that's all I've got to say!"

WONDERS OF THE ANIMAL KINGDOM

THE MONGOLIAN DEEP-FRIED BAT

This curious creature hides itself in the ceilings of fish and chip shops in North East Glasgow. When no one is looking, it will cover itself in batter and dive into the boiling fat. It then bides its time until some unsuspecting customer is about to place what they imagine is a nice piece of cod into their mouth, at that moment the Mongolian Deep-Fried Bat spreads its wings with a loud squeak, and flies out of their grasp to gasps of horror and the occasional heart attack.

No one knows why it does this.

THE FLEA THAT RAN SAINTSBURY'S

MR. SAINTSBURY (yes! the one who owns all the big grocery stores and hypermarkets – that Mr. Saintsbury!) once had a flea. I don't know where he'd got it from, for he is a most particular man and always washes behind his ears, and his stores, as you know, are a by-word for hygiene and cleanliness, but the impossible sometimes happens. The flea's name was Bertoldo. It was an Italian flea.

The curious thing is, however, that Mr. Saintsbury didn't know he'd got it. Now normally we know we've got a flea because we get bitten and we start scratching, and our mother usually says: "What's the matter with you, Terry? Have you got fleas?"

But Mr Saintsbury's flea was very careful never to bite Mr. Saintsbury.

When Bertoldo the Flea was feeling hungry, he would hop off Mr. Saintsbury and bite Mr. Saintsbury's dog. But he never ever bit Mr. Saintsbury himself.

This is the reason why.

The day that Bertoldo the Flea first landed on Mr. Saintsbury, Mr. Saintsbury was about to open the Biggest Supermarket In The World.

The moment he alighted on the great man's neck, Bertoldo could see that everybody was looking at him. Bertoldo was used to hopping from one person to another without anyone taking the slightest bit of notice. But here he was on Mr. Saintsbury, and everybody's eyes were upon him. Bertoldo raised a leg and waved to the crowd, and a little cheer went up. Bertoldo gave a deep bow, coughed and made this little speech.

"Ahem! Dear friends, I am aware that I am no ordinary flea. All my life I have known that I am destined for bigger things, and yet I have become used to being ignored... nobody seemed to notice I even existed. So your attention now is most welcome, for I have great things to say to you!"

Another cheer went up from the crowd, and Mr. Saintsbury, who had also been talking, scratched the top of his head – just where Bertoldo was standing – giving Bertoldo quite a fright. Bertoldo hopped down onto Mr. Saintsbury's ear.

"I think they're expecting us to cut that ribbon," whispered Bertoldo into Mr. Saintsbury's ear. "I'd do it myself, of course, only you've already got the scissors in your hand."

So Mr. Saintsbury cut the ribbon and the crowd cheered again, and Bertoldo the Flea took another bow. Then Mr. Saintsbury walked into the Biggest Supermarket In The World, and everyone followed. Bertoldo the Flea stood on the back of Mr. Saintsbury's collar, and addressed them:

"That's right! This way! Follow me!" And everybody did.

When they had walked right around the Biggest Supermarket In The World (which took quite a while) they reached the check-out till, and Bertoldo whispered into Mr. Saintsbury's ear:

"I think it would be a good idea if you bought something. It would be a symbolic gesture."

So Mr. Saintsbury bought some sausages for his supper, and then went outside and waved them at the crowd. Bertoldo the Flea took this chance to address the throng once more.

"Now the first thing I have to say to you is that you shouldn't waste your time here. What are you looking for? Happiness? Contentment? These are not things you can buy in a supermarket... not even the Biggest Supermarket In The World!"

Once again the people cheered, and Mr. Saintsbury waved his receipt. Bertoldo the Flea looked around with some satisfaction, and said to himself: "Well! I never thought everyone would agree so easily. Ahem!"

He cleared his throat and was just about to elaborate on the Nature of Happiness, when he noticed a particularly tasty-looking Red Setter sitting in the car park.

"Hang on a minute!" he shouted, and hopped across onto the Red Setter, and had a quick bite. He had filled up nicely and was beginning to feel slightly drowsy, when he suddenly realised the crowd was dispersing and Mr. Saintsbury was getting into his chauffeur-driven car.

Bertoldo only just made it back onto Mr. Saintsbury's collar in time, and as they drove out of the Largest Supermarket In The World, he remarked to Mr. Saintsbury: "Well, I suppose it's my fault for letting my attention wander... But it was a particularly ripe Red Setter. What kind of dogs do you like?"

Mr. Saintsbury, however, didn't reply, and so – feeling very pleased with himself – Bertoldo settled down for a nap.

Well, for the next few months, Bertoldo the Flea and Mr. Saintsbury did everything together.

Bertoldo gave Mr. Saintsbury advice on every occasion and Mr. Saintsbury seemed pretty happy to follow along. On one occasion Bertoldo advised Mr. Saintsbury – in no uncertain terms – not to open a hypermarket in Kilmarnock, but Mr. Saintsbury went ahead. And another time, Bertoldo tried to urge Mr. Saintsbury to stock pets as well as pet food, to no avail.

But generally speaking, Bertoldo the Flea was not at all surprised that Mr. Saintsbury took his advice on most matters of business and on one or two personal ones as well. And whenever Mr. Saintsbury made a public appearance, Bertoldo would take the opportunity

to impart some nugget of wisdom to the assembled throng. It always slightly niggled him that Mr. Saintsbury insisted on speaking at the same time, and once or twice, Bertoldo did ask him – very politely – to "Shut up!" But, on the whole, Bertoldo was satisfied that the superior content of his philosophical discourses would have made a greater impact on the crowd than Mr. Saintsbury's unexceptional remarks about the weather and the size of his supermarkets.

One day, however, it all went wrong.

Mr. Saintsbury and Bertoldo the Flea were sitting out in the garden, enjoying one of the last days of Summer. Bertoldo (who had rather changed his views on supermarkets) had been unfolding his Great Master Plan to Mr. Saintsbury.

"I believe we could turn the entire South East of England (including Basingstoke) into an autonomous, self-governing hypermarket," he said, "with a hundred mile car park covering most of Sussex. We could put every other shop in Britain out of business and draw our customers from as far North as Dingwall and as far West as Bude. I, of course, would remain as Managing Director, but you could be Chairperson without operational responsibilities..."

Well, it was a warm day, and when Bertoldo the Flea had finished outlining his grand scheme, he waited for Mr. Saintsbury to leap out of his deck chair and shout: "That's brilliant, Bertoldo! Let's start today!" But instead, all he got was a snore.

Bertoldo could scarcely believe his ears. In fact, he was so indignant, that for once, he forgot himself. He bit Mr. Saintsbury really hard – so hard in fact that Mr. Saintsbury woke up with a start.

"For goodness sake! Pay attention when I'm speaking to you!" exclaimed Bertoldo.

But Mr. Saintsbury wasn't listening. He went straight to the pet cupboard and got out a can of environmentally friendly spray. He looked at his dog and he said:

"Rover, old chap, I accuse you of having fleas!". And he sprayed Rover all over, and then sprayed himself.

And that was the end of Bertoldo... the flea that (for a few months) ran Saintsbury's.

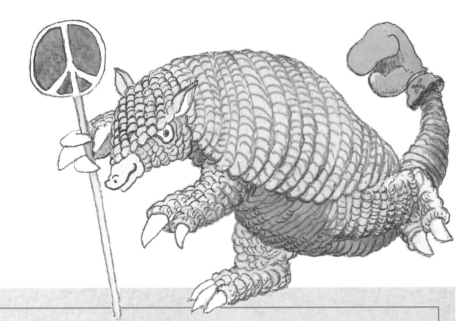

THE DISARMADILLO

This peace-loving mammal lacks the defensive plates found in other species of armadillo. As a result it is prey to any number of predators: wolves, coyotes, dogs, wildcats, bears etc. What is more, most armadillos, when startled by a predator, will jump three feet into the air, which so startles the predator that the armadillo has time to scuttle to safety. Unfortunately the Disarmadillo stands on one leg and pretends to be Dorothy in *The Wizard of Oz*, but as it doesn't have the ruby slippers, most wolves etc. fail to be convinced by the impression. When that strategy fails, the Disarmadillo will wander up to its predator and voluntarily climb into its mouth, rather than go through the motions of a long and nerve-wracking chase.

THE IMMORTAL JELLYFISH

THERE ARE TWO EXTRAORDINARY, unbelievably mind-boggling facts about jellyfish. The first is that there is one kind of jellyfish that lives forever, and that is what this story is about[1].

One day a vast crowd of herrings gathered around the Whale. The herrings were in a terrible tizzy, and they were all talking at once, until the Whale held up a flipper.

"I can't hear you if you all talk at once! Just one of you tell me what is the matter."

Of course this just increased the noise, as the herrings started arguing about who should be the spokesherring.

"Silence!" boomed the Whale, and he waited while all the herrings settled down.

"That's better!" boomed the Whale. "Now, *you!*" and he pointed to one herring out of all the thousands. "*You* tell me what you're all making such a fuss about."

"Asbut…trungling…ponkobands!" spluttered the herring.

"What?" boomed the Whale.

"You got him nervous…" explained the next herring along, "and we can't think when we're nervous, can we, herrings?"

"That's right!" chorused the other herrings, and they would have gone on agreeing about that for at least another half an hour, but the Whale held up his flipper.

"Very well," said the Whale, pointing to the herring that had just spoken. "You seem to be able to put two words together. You tell me what – under the sea – is the matter."

[1.] The jellyfish known as *Turritopis nutricula* starts out in life as a tiny jellyfish called a polyp. The polyp grows up into an adult jellyfish which mates and spawns like any other jellyfish. But then it gradually changes into a polyp. Once it reaches polyp stage it commences the cycle all over again. Hence scientists think that this particluar species of jellyfish may be immortal.

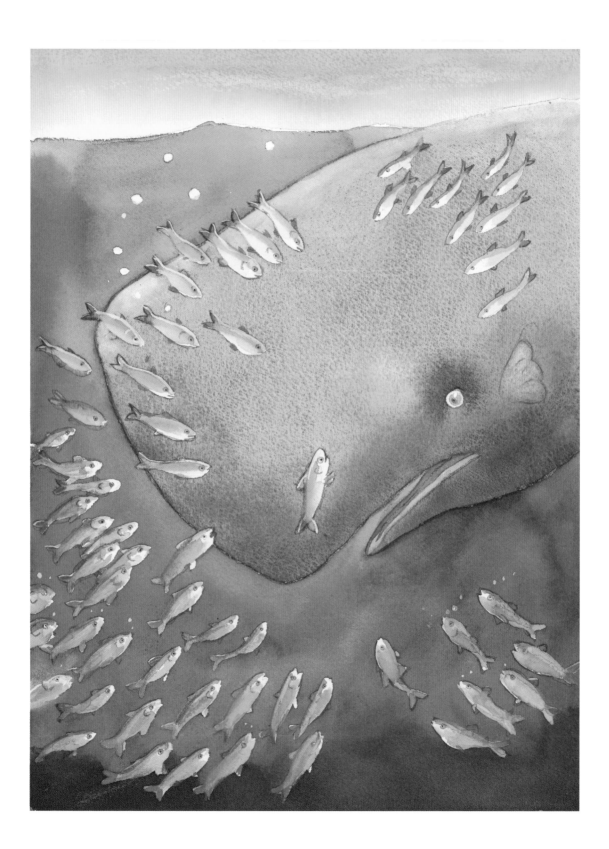

"Well," replied the herring. "It seems that men have started fishing for herring again!"

"So? What's new?" replied the Whale. "Men have been fishing the seas ever since they came into being."

"But! but! but! but! but! but!" chattered all the herrings together. "One at a time!" boomed the Whale. "You!" and he pointed to another herring.

"Plimplop!" blurted out the herring.

"You make us nervous when you point like that!" said the next herring along.

"All right," said the Whale, getting a touch exasperated. "You...you tell me!"

"Who? Me?" said the next herring along, looking about himself in alarm.

"Yes! You!" boomed the Whale. "You seem to have your wits about you. You act as spokesfish."

"But us herring only ever do things together!" said the next herring along.

"That's right!" chorused the rest, and the Whale held up his flipper before the other herrings say continue.

"I don't care!" boomed the Whale. "If you want me to listen to what you have to say, you will have to elect this herring as spokesfish."

"Spokesherring!" cried the other herrings in unison.

"Very well!" roared the Whale. "Spokesherring. Just get on with it!"

So the Spokesherring began, and as it spoke all the other herrings nodded in agreement. And this is what the Spokesherring said.

"Well in the old days men used nets with holes of such a size that even though they might catch us grown-up herrings, our small fry could wriggle through and escape. In this way there were always enough herrings to fill the oceans and carry on the proud tradition of the Herring Code..."

"Being Together, Swimming Together, Breaking Wind Together[2]!" chanted all the other herrings.

"But nowadays," continued the Spokesherring, "men are using nets with such a small mesh that they catch us all – adults and small fry alike. They will soon destroy all the herring in the sea."

"It's the same with us," cried the Cod and the Haddock, who had joined the Herring. "Men are behaving as if there were no tomorrow! They are dragging up the sea-bed itself,

[2] According to recent research, breaking wind is how herrings communicate amongst themselves. If you don't believe me, look up 'Herring farts' on the internet.

and when they do that, there is nothing left for the bottom-feeding fish to live on, and if the bottom-feeding fish cannot find their food they will die out, and if the bottom-feeding fish die out, so will those who live on the bottom-feeders and so on and so forth."

Just then a Turbot rose to speak. "Ahem!" he said. "I may be just a flat-fish, but… Have I just said that I'm a flat-fish or am I about to say it?"

"You just said it," said the other fish.

"Thank you," said the Turbot. "I get rather confused – it's having my eyes all on one side I think. Good morning."

"What were you going to say?" asked the Whale.

"Say?" said the Turbot. "I don't think I was going to 'say' anything."

"Then sit down!" roared the sea-lions.

"Except I should like to say: We need someone to warn Mankind that their insatiable greed is destroying all the life in the sea."

At this there was a general murmur of agreement from all the fish and shellfish and other creatures of the sea, whereupon the Turbot held up his flipper.

"Did I just say something?"

"Yes!" shouted all the other fish.

"Hello!" said the Turbot. "Buckingham Palace?"

"What we need," said the Whale, "is a fish that Men have respect for – a fish that can get Mankind to see sense. What about you dolphins – you get on well with Men?"

But the dolphins shook their heads. "For years we've been trying to warn Mankind about what they are doing to the sea, but they just think we want to play games and they keep throwing us balls and getting us to jump through hoops – which is, admittedly, fun."

"How about you sharks, then?" said the Whale.

"'Fraid not," said the sharks. "Humans panic as soon as we get near enough to reason to them. We'd never get them to see sense."

"It seems to me," said the Whale, "that we need the oldest and wisest creature in the ocean."

"The anchovies are pretty old," said a sea bream.

"Yes! We may not be very big but we can live as long as seven years!" exclaimed all the anchovies together. "Aren't we clever?"

"Cleverness has nothing to do with it," returned the Whale. "Besides men can live to 70 or 80 years. They're not going to be impressed by a clever seven year-old. What about the eels?"

"I've got an aunt who's 27," replied a conger eel.

"Still not long enough," said the Whale, shaking its great head. "What about you seals?"

"I'm 50!" replied one venerable seal.

"I'm 54!" said an even more venerable one.

"What about you, Whale?" said another seal. "Aren't you getting on for 100?"

"Yes! And men give you a lot of respect!" chorused the other fish.

The Whale sighed. "Oh Men talk and talk about how they respect us whales, but they still hunt and kill us. No! I'm scared of humans and I won't go near them."

Then the Learned Turtle spoke.

"I believe," it said, "there is a jellyfish that lives forever. His name is Turri Topsis. My Great Great Grandfather, who was also a Learned Turtle, told me that Old Turri Topsis was older than himself and older than anything else in the sea. "Yes sir!" he used to say to us young turtles, "Old Turri Topsis is immortal." We thought he was joking, but he wasn't."

"If there is any creature of the sea that will be able to impress Mankind," exclaimed the Whale, "it will certainly be a creature that has mastered the art of eternal life. Where can we find this jellyfish?"

"Follow me," said the Learned Turtle.

The Whale and the herrings, the cod and the haddock and all the other creatures of the sea followed the Learned Turtle until they came to a colony of jellyfish, that were drifting about off the coast of Ireland.

The Whale came straight to the point.

"Which one of you is the oldest?" he asked. The jellyfish all nodded at the largest of them.

"Is it true that you are millions of years old?" asked the Whale. And the large jellyfish nodded.

"In fact, not to beat about the bush," continued the Whale, "is it true that you are *immortal*?"

There was a deathly silence. Every creature held its breath and stared at the Ancient

Jellyfish: its transparent umbrella pulsed slightly and its tentacles waved as if searching for the answer, and then – just as a wave swept across the surface of the sea – it nodded gravely. Yes. It was!

The fish and the other sea creatures all thrashed their tails or span around and did somersaults in the water. Until the Whale called them all to order.

Then the Whale addressed the Immortal Jellyfish once more and told it how they wanted it to go and reason with Mankind.

"The whole future of the ocean and of every creature in the sea rests in your tentacles," said the Whale. "Will you take on this grave responsibility?"

Once again there was a silence, and not a creature in the sea dared to breathe. The Immortal Jellyfish seemed to be considering for a long, long time, but finally it nodded.

The Whale and the herring, the cod and the haddock and all the other creatures of the sea heaved a sigh of relief.

"Thank you," said the Whale. "We shall await your return and may the Spirit of the Ocean bring you success, and enable you to persuade Mankind to reform his ways."

Then he turned to the other sea creatures and announced in his booming voice: "We shall leave this matter in the tentacles of our venerable brother the Immortal Jellyfish. We shall all meet again, when he returns from his mission."

Then he turned once more to the Immortal Jellyfish and said: "Good luck, O Wonderous Jellyfish!"

The Immortal Jellyfish nodded sagely and all the creatures of the sea swam off their different ways, and the other jellyfish nodded after them and waved their tentacles.

But the Whale never re-called the meeting, and the herrings and the cod and the haddock never met again. In fact, they are still waiting for the Immortal Jellyfish to report back. For I'm afraid I have to tell you that the Immortal Jellyfish never managed to persuade human beings that they should not destroy the ocean bed. In fact the Immortal Jellyfish didn't even try to make contact with Mankind. In fact it never even set out on its mission! Indeed, to tell you the truth, although it was such an ancient jellyfish and although it had lived in the ocean for possibly millions of years, it didn't really understand what it had been asked to do. In fact, it didn't really understand a word that had been said to it.

Do you remember that I said that there are two extraordinary, unbelievably mind-boggling facts about jellyfish? Well, the first is that there is one kind of jellyfish that is immortal, but the second extraordinary, unbelievably mind-boggling fact is that no jellyfish has a brain. So it doesn't matter if they do live forever – they never get any wiser.

WONDERS OF THE ANIMAL KINGDOM

THE SOUTH AFRICAN TALKING TOAD

The only amphibian that can be trained to say simple words and phrases. Unfortunately these toads speak English with such a thick Afrikaans accent that it is impossible to understand them. However this is probably as well because, being toads, they are extremely rude creatures. They love shouting insults at passing vicars, jeering at Her Majesty the Queen, and talking endlessly about bottoms.

THE RULE OF THE LION

A LONG, LONG TIME AGO, King of the Jungle summoned the Lord High Wildebeest and the Prince of the Striped Gazelles to appear before him.

The Lord High Wildebeest visited the Prince of the Striped Gazelles and said: "Prince! What do you think? Should we go and appear before the King of the Jungle as he has commanded?"

"Of course!" replied the Prince of the Striped Gazelles.

"But you know that Lion likes nothing better than a fat wildebeest like me or a striped gazelle like you for supper."

"But Lion is an honourable beast," replied the Prince of the Striped Gazelles. "He would not try to trick us."

"Perhaps you are right," said the Lord High Wildebeest.

And so the Lord High Wildebeest and the Prince of the Striped Gazelles made the journey across the hot plains to the canyon where the King of the Jungle lived.

"You are welcome!" said Lion. "I have called you both before me because I have some important news for you.

"I wish to create a world in which we all live together in peace. So I propose to make it a law that, in future, instead of hunting you down and killing you for our supper, we lions will help protect all you wildebeest and striped gazelles against your enemies. We will seek out the best grass for you, and we will escort you there to stop the leopards and the spotted hyenas from attacking you.

"All I ask in return is that you wildebeest and striped gazelles make a solemn promise never to attack us lions in future.

"So go and gather your families and friends and relations and bring them here to the safety of this canyon, and I will post two lions to guard each entrance to guarantee your safety."

When the lion had finished speaking, there was a silence. Then the Prince of the Striped Gazelles spoke up.

"Your Majesty," he said. "You have always been regarded as the most honourable and just of animals. We striped gazelles thank you with all our stripes."

Then he bowed low to the King of the Jungle. And so did the Lord High Wildebeest. After which, the Lord High Wildebeest and the Prince of the Striped Gazelles took their leave of the King of the Jungle and went back to join their families and friends and relations. But on the way, the Lord High Wildebeest stopped the Prince of the Striped Gazelles in a secret place where no lions could hear them, and said:

"Prince, my heart is full of misgivings. How can we be sure we can trust Lion?"

"Of all animals Lion is the most honourable," replied the Prince of the Striped Gazelles. "He is so strong and powerful he does not have to rely on tricks to catch his supper."

"But supposing this particular lion has become old and lazy and doesn't want to chase around to catch his supper?" said the Lord High Wildebeest.

"You heard what the King of the Jungle said!" exclaimed the Prince of the Striped Gazelles. "He will make it law that no lion may attack us. Instead the lions will protect us. He is going to put two lions on guard at each end of the canyon to keep our enemies out."

"But tell me this," said the Lord High Wildebeest, "what is there in this arrangement that benefits the lion?"

"Well," replied the Prince of the Striped Gazelles, "his law forbids wildebeest and striped gazelles from attacking lions."

"But never in the history of the world," pointed out the Lord High Wildebeest, "has a wildebeest or a striped gazelle attacked a lion,"

"But just imagine!" cried the Prince of the Striped Gazelles, "We will never have to trek across the hot plain in search of the best grass again – it will all be found for us! We shall be able to live and feed without fear and without forever watching the horizon for danger! Can you imagine anything more wonderful?"

"Hmmm," muttered the Lord High Wildebeest.

"I shall call together all the herds of striped gazelles from over the hot plains and bring them here where they will be safe," said the Prince of the Striped Gazelles.

And with that the Prince of the Striped Gazelles galloped across the hot plains and sought out all the herds of striped gazelles, and led every single one of them back to Lion's Canyon.

But the Lord High Wildebeest returned to his herd on the hot plain and said not a word. Which is why to this day, the wildebeest still live in fear of lions and other predators, as they roam across the hot plains seeking the good grass.

And it is also why not a single striped gazelle exists today.

THE TOAD ROAD

A MAN ONCE CAME TO SETTLE IN A BEAUTIFUL VALLEY. He decided to build his house near a pleasant pond where lilies grew in abundance and where herons came to fish for their supper.

"Adam," said his neighbour, who ran a small café nearby. "You better not build your house there,

"Why ever not?" said Adam. "I can build my house where I like."

"But you'll be building your house right across the Toad Road," replied the man who ran the café.

"What do you mean?" asked Adam.

"Well," said his neighbour, "every year toads come in their hundreds to return to the pond where they were born. They come to spawn, and they always take the same road. So don't build your house there."

"I shall do as I like," said Adam. "The toads can walk around my house,"

And so Adam built his house across the Toad Road.

That spring, when all the toads came tramping from miles away to return to the pond where they were born, they found Adam's house blocking their way. Now you might have thought, as Adam thought, that the toads would simply go round the house, but that isn't what toads do. The toads simply *wouldn't* change their route for anybody or for anything. So they found ways through Adam's house, under the floorboards and across the kitchen and down the hallway and under the front door.

"Adam!" screamed his wife. "There's thousands of toads tramping through our house! I'm not going to stay here!"

"I'll put a stop to them," replied Adam. And he set to work to make it impossible for the toads to come through the house on their way back after the spawning season.

But it didn't work. When the toads came back from spawning and found they couldn't get in under the front door or up through the floorboards, they simply climbed the walls

of the house and tramped across the roof and down the other side.

"Arrgggh!" screamed Adam's wife. "There are millions of toads climbing all over our house! I'm not staying here a moment longer!" And she ran out of the house and slammed the door.

"I'm not letting a few toads turn me out of house and home!" exclaimed Adam.

And all that summer he made traps and snares to catch the toads. And when they returned the next spring, Adam caught them in his traps and snares and put them all into sacks which he threw in the back of his car and then drove for 300 miles. When he thought he was far enough away from home, he stopped the car, took out the sacks and released the toads. For he was not a cruel man. He just thought he could do as he liked.

Then he drove the 300 miles back to his home in the beautiful valley, feeling certain he'd seen the last of those toads.

But the toads weren't going to let a few hundred miles stop them getting to the place where they wanted to spawn, and so straight away, without waiting for the spawning season, they started to make their way south. All that summer there were reports of an army of toads marching through the countryside, and naturalists from all over the world came to see them.

Eventually the television news started to film their progress southwards, and all the time everyone was trying to guess where they were heading.

"Toads often make long journeys to return to the place of their origin," said a TV reporter. "But nothing like this has been seen before: these toads are moving at the wrong time of year and travelling too far. and still the big question is: where are they heading?"

Well, the toads took their time, crawling at a leisurely pace, as toads do, and all through the summer, viewers turned on the TV to follow their progress.

One or two of the toads became quite famous. There was one they nick-named 'Winston'. He was the biggest of the toads and appeared to be some sort of leader. Then there was 'Chalky' who had a white splodge in the middle of his back, and who always seemed to be getting left behind, but who always managed to catch up somehow or other. Then there was a young female toad, whom the reporters nick-named 'Doris' who was always stopping in the middle of the road and causing traffic to swerve to avoid her.

Eventually, of course, the toads arrived at the house of Adam. And so did the television crews.

The toads were tired and footsore, and they were late for their spawning, but they were determined to get to their pond, and – what's more – they were determined to take the Toad Road that led through Adam's house.

Adam was equally determined to stop them. He too had been following the News reports of the toads' progress, and when they arrived outside his house he was ready for them. He had laid out his traps and snares and done everything to make sure the toads would not get through, and this time, he was determined, was going to be the last time the toads would ever get the chance to try.

And so it was that millions of television viewers watched aghast as these famous toads – the Heroes of The Long March – were trapped and ensnared by a grumpy-looking man with a sack and a shovel.

Millions of television viewers watched in sheer disbelief, as the grumpy-looking man picked up the Celebrated Leader of the Heroes of the Long March – Winston the Toad himself – and, instead of presenting him with a medal or shaking his foreleg, the grumpy-looking man threw the Great Leader into his sack.

"Stop that!" cried a Naturalist. "Put that *Bufo terrestris* down this instant!"

"What the devil are you talking about?" growled Adam, who thought it was bad enough having toads turning up unannounced on his doorstep – let alone television crews.

"That toad in your hand, sir!" exclaimed the Naturalist. "Please put it down before you do it some harm!"

"It's going in the sack with the rest of 'em!" said Adam, and he threw toad into the sack.

"Wasn't that Doris?" exclaimed a Lady News Reporter who had just joined the Naturalist.

"Yes!" exclaimed TV News Director. "And that's Chalky!" he cried, pointing at the toad that Adam now had in his hand.

"Clear off! The lot of you!" shouted Adam. "This is private property and you are trespassing – same as these toads!"

"Those toads have the right to go wherever they want!" shouted the Naturalist.

"What are you going to do with those toads?" asked the Lady Reporter.

"That's none of your business," replied Adam.

"He's going to kill them!" shouted the Naturalist.

"After they've marched so far!" exclaimed several of the TV people.

"Chalky has worked so hard to catch up with the others!" cried cried the Lady Presenter's Personal Assistant.

"And poor Doris!" shouted the Sound Recordist. "To escape death on the motorway so many times and then end up in a sack!"

"It's not right!" they all shouted together, and so did half a million viewers, sitting in front of their television sets. "He can't be allowed to get away with that!" And the television viewers leapt out of their comfy chairs, and jumped into their cars and raced to the beautiful valley, with tyres screeching and engines roaring, filling the beautiful valley with fumes from their exhaust pipes. Then they swarmed around the house that Adam had built across the Toad Road.

First of all they shook the doors. Then they started banging on the windows. Then they climbed onto the roof and started tearing off the tiles. And do you know what? By the end of the day there was nothing left of Adam's house: it was lying in pieces across the Toad Road.

The toads were all released and finally made it to the pond where they were born. There they spawned and the next year there were more toads than ever in the beautiful valley.

As for Adam, well he was never seen again. He probably still thinks he can do as he likes, but I can tell you one thing: he's never ever built another house anywhere within sight of a Toad Road.

SWEET AND SOUR WALLABIES

These loveable little creatures are a firm favourite with children, parents and the hard-of-hearing. They bounce all over your plate, providing hours of hilarious fun for the kids, and a moment of relaxation for parents. The hard-of-hearing also appreciate the loud shouts and piercing screams of the children as they stab each other with their forks, in their vain attempts to catch their dinner.

THE PENGUIN
WITHOUT A NAME

IN THE EMPTY WASTES OF THE ANTARCTIC, where the wind blasts across the ice and there is more sleet in the air than air, a small penguin was standing with his back to the icy gusts. The snow was piling up on its back, and rapidly turning to ice. The penguin just stood there, with its head down.

Just then a kindlier wind happened to blow past, and it noticed how miserable the penguin looked. So it circled around the penguin and said these words.

"What's the matter, little penguin? You look so sad."

The penguin looked up for a moment and said "Humph!" and then it looked down again, as the kindlier wind circled around and around it.

"Tell me," said the wind.

"What?" asked the penguin.

"What makes you so sad?" asked the kindlier wind.

"Well look at this place," snorted the penguin. "Look at these empty wastes. Nothing but ice and snow for thousands of miles. Icy mountains. Icy plains. Nothing but emptiness and cold and darkness."

"This is the Antarctic," said the kindlier wind. "This is what it's like."

"And look at me," returned the penguin. "I have nothing. No home. No parents. No children. No possessions. No friends. Nothing. I don't even have a name. How more truly miserable could a creature be?"

The wind wound around the penguin and ruffled its smooth feathers just ever so slightly.

"Walk on," whispered the wind. "I will go with you."

"Walk?" exclaimed the penguin. "I can only waddle. Look at me! I'm a bird and yet I can't even fly! I'm not made for this vast emptiness."

"Walk on," whispered the wind again. "I will go with you, and let us see what we shall see."

So the penguin reluctantly started to waddle across the vast emptiness of ice and snow that is the Antarctic.

Eventually they came to the edge of a cliff.

"What do you see?" asked the wind.

"I see a vast plain of nothingness. Ice and snow and blasting wind. Nothing else."

"Perhaps your name is Eric?" said the wind.

"I don't have a name," retorted the penguin. "I don't have anything."

So the wind led the penguin on. They took a path that went down the side of the cliff, and soon they were at the bottom,

"What do you see now?" asked the wind.

"I see the same," replied the penguin. "There is nothing. I have nothing. Not even a name."

"Perhaps your name is Arbuthnot?" said the wind.

"No. I don't have a name," answered the penguin. "How many more times do I have to tell you?"

So the wind led the little penguin on across the wind-swept plain, over the drifts of snow, over the occasional crevice and round the snow-strewn rocks that stuck up out of the ice. Eventually they came to the edge of the sea.

"Now what do you see?" asked the kindlier wind.

"Nothing," said the penguin. "I see dark, cold, cold water stretching as far as the eye can see into the gloomy distance. Nothing but icy water and waves. Nothing."

"Jump," said the kindler wind.

"What?!" exclaimed the penguin. "It's bad enough here on dry land! I'm not going to get wet through and colder than I already am!"

"Jump!" said the wind again.

"Not on your life!" exclaimed the penguin. "There's leopard seals in there, lying in wait under the ice, that would eat me up with six little bites. There are orcas and sea lions that would guzzle me up without thinking twice."

"You are right," whispered the wind. "The sea is a dangerous place for you penguins.

On the land, you have no enemies, and so you can afford to just waddle your way along without having to rush. What a luxury!"

"I'd be crazy to leap in there!" exclaimed the penguin.

"Hold out your flippers," whispered the wind.

"What for?"

"Just hold them out. That's right" And as the penguin held out his flippers, the kindly wind blew a gust that was so strong it knocked the penguin head over heels and it tumbled into the cold Antarctic sea.

And the strange thing is, the moment it was under the waves, the penguin suddenly felt happy for the first time in its life. It didn't feel cold, because its feathers kept a layer of warm air around its body. And it found it could move so easily through the waters that it was better than flying.

The kindly wind watched the penguin diving down a hundred feet or more until it disappeared in the gloomy depths of the Antarctic Sea. Then suddenly it was zooming back up again until it broke the surface with a fish in its mouth.

"What's your name?" called the wind.

"Sea-Bird!" shouted the penguin, and swallowed the fish.

THE MAHATMA STAGE ANT

This obnoxious insect is considered a pest throughout the subcontinent. Not only does it bore through all woodwork in theatres (making the stages spectacularly unsafe) it also takes over entire productions with self-indulgent and bombastic interpretations of the major classical roles.

On one occasion the ants reduced *Titus Andronicus* to the battle sequences, and managed to drag them out for four hours, prompting one critic to remark that if he saw one more dismembered head or another twisted thorax he would personally come and stamp on every ant on stage. On another occasion, they turned a perfectly adequate production of *Othello* into a travesty by playing Desdemona as Mrs Potato Head from *Toy Story 2* and Othello as the Donkey in *Shrek*. "The ants totally missed the sublime passion of Shakespeare's tragedy," complained one critic. "By representing Iago as Father Christmas," wrote another, "the ants turned what should have been a profoundly moving theatrical experience into the equivalent of a visit to Santa's Grotto."

These are said to be the only representatives of the animal kingdom that Ghandi was tempted to tread on.

THE IMAGINARY DRAGON

A DRAGON WAS ONCE TAKING AFTERNOON TEA with his friend the Gryphon. "What the devil's the matter with you, Dragon?" exclaimed the Gryphon, who was never in the best of moods. "You look as if you'd swallowed a hedgehog!"

"I wish I had," murmured the Dragon.

"Balderdash!" exclaimed the Gryphon. "Nobody could possibly want to swallow a hedgehog!"

"I might feel better than I do now," said the Dragon.

"You make me cross!" exclaimed the Gryphon, who was always cross anyway. "I can't stand you being miserable! It's like sitting opposite a road accident!"

"Sorry!" said the Dragon.

"All right! All right!" said the Gryphon irritably. "You'd better tell me what's wrong."

"You'll only laugh," replied the Dragon.

"Of course I won't," grumbled the Gryphon, frowning even more than usual. "Scout's honour!"

"Well…" said the Dragon cautiously, and he looked hard at the Gryphon with his old, sad eyes. "I think I may not exist."

By the time the Gryphon had stopped laughing, the Dragon was on his way home, and the Gryphon had to run to catch his friend up.

"Come back, Dragon!" roared the Gryphon. "You can't leave a perfectly good cup of tea half drunk!"

Now even though the Dragon had been looking so miserable, he had been enjoying that cup of tea, so he eventually allowed the Gryphon to persuade him to return to the tea table, and they carried on where they had left off.

"Where the devil did you get a tom-fool notion like that from?" asked the Gryphon in his gruff way.

"Well," replied the Dragon. "I was reading this book that said dragons are mythological creatures — that is they are imaginary creatures that don't actually exist!"

"Horse-feathers!" exclaimed the Gryphon. "You're sitting here having tea with me! How could you possibly not exist?"

"Well," said the Dragon slowly, "suppose that I were just a product of your imagination? You're just imagining I'm sitting here having tea with you?"

"But…but…but…" stuttered the Gryphon, who was by this time was becoming even more irritated than normal. "I've never heard such arrant nonsense in my life!" And he punched the Dragon right on the nose.

"Ow!" exclaimed the Dragon, holding his nose, which is always the tenderest part of a dragon. "What did you do that for?"

"To prove to you that you are not the product of my imagination!" exclaimed the Gryphon. "If you were an imaginary creature you wouldn't be able to feel anything when I punched you on the nose. You wouldn't feel anything, see anything or hear anything!"

The Dragon looked at the Gryphon with his old, sad eyes, and thought for a long time — possibly a couple of hundred years — and then finally said:

"How do we know?"

"How do we know?! How do we know?!" exclaimed the Gryphon, whose tea had gone cold while he was waiting for the Dragon to reply. "What the devil are you wittering on about now, Dragon? How do we know what?"

"How do we know," replied the Dragon, "that imaginary creatures — creatures that somebody has imagined and created — can't feel and see and hear?"

"Well it's obvious they can't!" exclaimed the Gryphon. "If they've just been created out of thin air how could they possible feel or see or hear?"

"But everybody and everything has been created in one way or another…" replied the Dragon.

'BUT YOU'RE SITTING HERE TALKING TO ME!" exploded the Gryphon who by this time had had more than enough of this conversation.

The Dragon looked at him with his old, sad eyes and said:

"Ah! That's the problem. How do we know that this whole event — me sitting here having tea with you — hasn't been made up by somebody, who has then written it down on a bit of paper?"

"I can't stand all this nonsense!" exclaimed the exasperated Gryphon. "Look! We'll find somebody else, who will be able to confirm that we do exist!"

So they went to the Unicorn.

"Unicorn!" exclaimed the Gryphon in his gruff way, "Dragon here thinks he may not exist – that he may be just an imaginary creature that somebody dreamed-up! Tell him that he's real!" But the Unicorn looked rather doubtful.

"Oh dear!" he said. "That's serious! If Dragon isn't real, perhaps none of us are!"

"Absolute piffle!" roared the Gryphon. "You're all talking Twaddle! Bunkum and Tommyrot! I won't listen to this drivel a moment longer!"

"Unicorn has a point," said the Dragon.

"Very well," grumbled the Gryphon, "we'll go ask the Sphinx!"

"But you know the Sphinx's answers often create more problems than the original question," ventured the Unicorn.

"But sometimes," said the Gryphon, "those new problems help you to solve the original problem."

So the three friends went along to the Sphinx, and the Gryphon said: "Look here, Sphinx, my two friends have got some tom-fool notion in their heads that they don't exist. They think they might be imaginary creatures that someone has dreamt up."

"In fact," said the Dragon, "this whole conversation may have been made up by somebody and written down on a bit of paper."

"How can we be sure it isn't?" asked the Unicorn. "How can we be sure that we exist?"

The three friends waited for the Sphinx to answer. But the Sphinx took his time – perhaps a couple of thousand years – before he finally opened his mouth, and a huge booming voice echoed over the desert sands.

The three friends trembled, as they heard the Sphinx's words:

"Nothing exists," said the Sphinx.

Well the three friends were so bemused by the Sphinx's answer they didn't know what to say. But they didn't want to prolong the conversation for another two thousand years, so they said:

"Thank you very much, Sphinx, very helpful," and walked back across the burning desert sands.

"Well that didn't get us anywhere!" exclaimed the Gryphon. "What a waste of two thousand years!"

"If nothing exists, then *we* certainly don't exist!" said the Unicorn dismally. "It's really most unsettling to think that we are all just imaginary characters in somebody else's story!"

"Yes!" agreed the Dragon. "It's even worse than I feared. It's not just me – *nothing* exists!"

The three friends walked on in the silence of Dreamland, until all at once the Dragon stopped and sat down.

"Wait a minute!" he cried. "I've just had a thought!" And then he started laughing and laughing.

Well of course the Gryphon got very annoyed.

"What the devil are you laughing at, Dragon?" he said.

"Yes!" exclaimed the Unicorn. "How can you laugh? If nothing exists and we are all just imaginary things – it's nothing to laugh about!" And the Unicorn and the Gryphon stared at the Dragon as if he were quite mad.

"But don't you see?" exclaimed the Dragon. "The Sphinx's answer solves the problem!"

"What the devil are you talking about?" growled the Gryphon.

"Yes!" said the Unicorn. "Explain yourself!"

"Well," said the Dragon, "it cannot be that nothing exists, as the Sphinx well knows, because if we were all imaginary creatures and this whole story were the product of somebody else's imagination – then at least we know for certain that imagination exists! And as long as imagination exists then we exist even if we're imaginary!"

And the three friends, the Dragon, the Gryphon and the Unicorn sat there in the vast plain of Dreamland, laughing and laughing, until the sun set, and they went home to dream their own dreams.

THE BOTTOM-FEEDING WARTHOG

This curious creature feeds by sitting on its food, which it then ingests through its bottom. Since its principle diet consists of caviar mixed with a little *foie gras* and washed down with a bottle of the best Champagne, it has considerable difficulty in finding enough to eat. It can be seen hanging around street corners, swearing at passing sailors and demanding rent-free accommodation for playwrights. No one knows why.

The Bottom-Feeding Warthog is doubly unlucky: it cannot taste the fine food and drink it lives on, and, since it excretes via its mouth, the process is always accompanied by mournful cries of disgust. It regards itself as the most unfortunate of animals and is prone to serious bouts of depression.

It is also the single biggest argument against evolution.

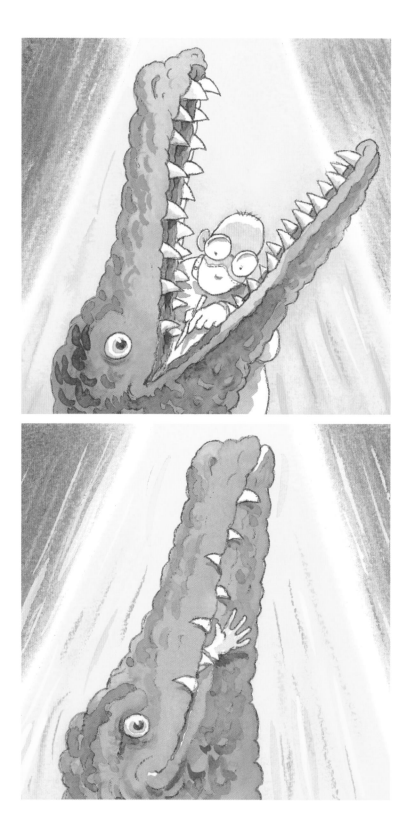